MW00981113

WEET ALONE

BY JOHN WILSON

ILLUSTRATIONS BY JANICE ARMSTRONG

Napoleon Publishing

Cover art: Alan Barnard

Le Conseil des Arts du Canada depuis 1957 | The Canada Council for the Arts since 1957

Napoleon Publishing gratefully acknowledges the support of the Canada Council for the Arts for our publishing program.

Napoleon Publishing
Toronto, Ontario, Canada

Printed in Canada

05 04 03 02 01 00 99   5 4 3 2 1

Canadian Cataloguing in Publication Data

Wilson, John (John Alexander), 1951-
        Weet alone

ISBN 0-929141-68-7

I. Armstrong, Janice-   II. Title.

PS8595.I5834W43   1999   jC813'.54   C99-931191-3
PZ7.W6964We 1999

For my mother,
whom I once asked hopefully,
"Do you remember the dinosaurs?"

CHAPTER 1

on the beach

The world was going mad, and it was doing it very noisily. Large chunks of rock were crashing through the branches of the trees and embedding themselves in the ground. Some were landing offshore, sending up tall columns of water and steam which stood like pillars for impossible moments before falling back into the turbulent sea. The sound was almost deafening, but it could not quite block out the screams of the birds and animals who were caught up in this madness.

In the midst of all the turmoil, a terrified Weet stood frozen, his arms wrapped around Saar. He wanted to run, but could think of nowhere to run to. Danger was everywhere. He could see Eric and Rose struggling towards him. Freeing one hand, he reached out to pull his friends closer. Before he could make contact, a violent crash hurled Weet and Saar painfully backwards against the trunk of a large tree. Eric and Rose disappeared in a cloud of dust and flying debris.

Weet's head was spinning. What was happening?

WILSON

It felt like the end of the world. Gradually, he realized that the awful noises had stopped. Opening his eyes, he looked around.

The violence had ended, and the scene was bathed in an uncanny silence. Splintered trees and torn vegetation covered the ground. A thick pall of dust hung in the air, thrown up from craters that were everywhere. Through the dust, Weet could just make out figures getting gingerly to their feet. Their groans and whistles for help reached his ringing ears. Weet turned to Saar. She was conscious and appeared unhurt.

"Are you all right?" she asked.

"Yes," Weet replied, "I think so. Are you?"

Saar nodded.

"We must help the others," she said, getting to her feet.

Weet struggled upright and followed her. Every muscle in his body hurt, but as he moved through the shattered trees, he realized how lucky he and Saar were. Many people had been killed or injured. There was a lot to be done to help the injured. To Weet's relief, his pet, Sinor, was unhurt. Soron, Saar's father, had a broken arm, but once it was splinted and bound with creepers, he was able to help organize care of the more seriously hurt. Gradually, some semblance of order was created from the chaos and fear, but it was not until mid-afternoon that Weet could stop and gather his thoughts. They were still confused, but they were dominated by one fact. Although he had been looking all day, Weet had found not the slightest trace of Eric, Rose or Sally.

A small wave rose, ran up the beach in a flurry of pebbles, and broke over Eric's new sneakers. Roused from his reverie, the boy looked down and stepped back.

"If the tide weren't coming in, you'd stand there all day dreaming." Eric's sister Rose was behind him, standing on a large boulder. She was dressed in floral shorts and a T-shirt printed with eleven white sheep and one black one.

"I was thinking," he said.

"About Weet?" Rose asked as she jumped off the rock and walked over to stand beside her brother.

Eric picked up a piece of driftwood and threw it out to sea. Sally bounded past him and hurled herself into the water to retrieve it.

"Yeah," he said at length. "I wonder how he is?"

It must have been the thousandth time Eric had asked himself that question in the ten days since the car had almost crashed on the way out to

WILSON

Vancouver. Christmas, with all its excitement and festivities, had come and gone, and there were only three days left until they had to set off back across the mountains to cold, snowy Alberta. The weather had been mild, even for the west coast, with several sunny days when the temperature had climbed into the teens. Eric's father had said it was because this was a particularly strong El Niño year. Eric found it difficult to fully believe that a water current off the coast of Peru, thousands of miles away, could produce warm, holiday weather in Vancouver, but (if that were true) it was just one more piece of evidence that the climate was changing.

Today was the warmest day so far, and this explained the children's presence on Kitsilano Beach. Eric watched as Sally, with only her head showing above the water, grabbed the stick, turned, and began the long swim back to shore. Behind her, the Coast Mountains stood large and snow-capped, in stark contrast to the quiet hills that would have made up the view in Weet's time.

"Do you think the meteor shower that sent us back here from Weet's time was the one that killed the dinosaurs?" Rose asked him for the hundredth time, but Eric didn't mind. It was a question he couldn't get out of his mind either. Had the shower of meteors, which had seemed so

dangerous and threatening on the island, merely been the landing of a few specks of cosmic dust, flaked off from the huge lump of rock which had crashed with almost unimaginable force into what is now Mexico? The giant meteor's impact had ended most of the life on the planet, and possibly Weet's. Eric laughed ironically. "I don't know," he said.

Rose glanced up at the calm blue sky. "It's hard to believe that there's a big chunk of rock up there that might hit us."

"Actually," Eric responded, "there are thousands of them, and some come very close. In 1990, there was an asteroid that only missed us by six hours. And there have been cases of big ones exploding over Siberia, the Amazon and the Pacific Ocean. It's only since people have started looking for them that we've begun to realize how common they are. Somebody worked out that your chances of being killed by a catastrophic impact are about the same as dying in a plane crash." Eric lowered his gaze back to the beach.

"You know," he said, "the first time we went back in time, I spent hours worrying that the meteor we had seen in the badlands had been big enough to destroy the world and kill Mom and Dad. Now I can't stop worrying that the meteor we saw in Weet's world killed him."

"Well, we'll have to go back and find out." Rose

looked so matter-of-fact and serious that Eric had to swallow the comment he was going to make about Rose controlling time travel. "How?" was all he could manage.

"Remember yesterday, when we went to the Anthropology Museum, and that man told me not to touch the old carving of the bear?"

Their conversation was interrupted by a very wet Sally dropping her stick and shaking herself violently at their feet. The children retreated from the flying spray. Eric bent to retrieve the stick and flung it as far as he could along the beach. Sally raced off gleefully.

"Yes," he answered, "the man said it was over a hundred years old and that the moisture and oils from your hand would make it rot."

"Well," Rose continued, "I was making a wish."

This time Eric couldn't control himself. "It wasn't a wishing bear," he smiled.

"I know," said Rose, unperturbed, "but he looked so old and cracked and—friendly, that I just had to reach out and touch his head and ask him to help us get back to Weet."

Rose picked up a pebble and skimmed it over the water.

"Well, it can't hurt," said her brother. "Still, if we do go back again, I wonder how it will happen this time, and I wonder what we'll find there. You know, before any of this happened, I'd have given my right arm to travel back in time to the Age of Dinosaurs to see what they really looked like. Now I'm not so sure I want to go back. Oh, I'd love to see Weet again, but it always turns out to be a lot more complicated than I imagine. I guess any age has its problems, not just ours."

The pair made their way back up the beach in silence, followed by the bedraggled dog. At the top, they stopped by a table-like shelf of rock. It looked like pebbly concrete, but Eric knew from his reading that it was conglomerate and that the pebbles in it had been washed down from the first rising of the mountains to the north, right at the end of the reign of the dinosaurs. It was a connection to Weet. Perhaps the very pebbles he was looking at were tumbling down some gully or washing along a beach at the very time that Weet and Saar were trying to decide what to do after the velociraptor attack on the tree city. Gently he ran his hand over the dark, smooth surfaces of the pebbles.

"Come on," Eric said, moving towards the car park, "we'd better get back. I still have to get my stuff together for the ski trip tomorrow. Race you to the car."

The two children, with a barking Sally at their heels, pounded across the asphalt towards the waiting car.

CHAPTER 2

the ski trip

The sun was shining, but there was little warmth in it today. It hung low in the sky and looked washed-out through a layer of high cloud and haze which threatened to obscure it. Eric shivered, and not just from the cold. The drive up to Whistler Ski Resort had unsettled him more than he cared to admit. The journey in the half-light of dawn along the winding mountain road had brought back unpleasant memories. At every corner Eric had tensed, half-expecting blinding lights to suddenly appear around the bend. Nothing had happened, and they had arrived safely, but the experience was unnerving. Even Rose had been unusually quiet.

The problem was made worse by Eric's inactivity on the ski slope. He had to look after Rose on the nursery hill, and that mostly involved sitting watching her. Eric had tried a few times to join her, but the slope was so gradual that he couldn't get up any speed, and even if he had been able to, he would have had to spend all his time looking out for small kids with no sense of direction or control.

So here he sat at the edge of the slope, watching his sister tire herself out. At least she was keeping warm. Rose must have been up and down the slope fifteen times already, and she wasn't showing any sign of tiring yet. The reason she needed watching was that each time she trekked up, she attempted to edge a little higher. The screen of trees prevented her, but once she had tried to sneak across to the intermediate slope, forcing Eric to go after her and argue her back. That had been difficult, because she was only going where he wanted to go. But his parents had been specific: Rose was not to go off the nursery slope. After lunch, his Mom would take over with Rose and he and his Dad could be more adventurous. But the slopes would be crowded by the afternoon and, in any case, Eric would probably freeze to death before then.

Eric was leaning against a tree at the top of the slope. He had a good view of the slope and of Rose. Just a few feet behind him, through the trees, was the lot where the car was parked. Sally lay at his feet. Her leash was around the tree trunk, but Eric had loosened her collar when he came up to keep her company.

Sally hated being cooped up for long periods. Once, to protest a long day in the car, she had systematically destroyed a foam camping pillow while they had all been having dinner. They returned to find the pillow reduced to inch-sized fragments which, because of their static charge, clung to every surface of the car. Everyone had spent the rest of the holiday picking green foam off their clothes and the car upholstery. Even now, three years later, bits of foam still turned up in odd corners when the car seats were cleaned. Ever since then, Eric had tried to get her out of the car as much as possible.

Animals weren't allowed on the ski slopes, but he rationalized that the trees weren't actually on the slopes proper, and no one had said anything yet. Right now, Sally was chewing ice balls off her feet.

Rose was falling down more now—she must be getting tired. Eric did not regard that prospect with relish. Recently, Rose had matured. There were fewer tantrums, and it was possible to have a civilized conversation with her. Eric was beginning to feel that she was more of a companion than a little sister. The exception was when Rose got tired. Then she reverted back to all the irrationality that Eric disliked in little kids. If she was getting tired already, the rest of the morning would not be fun. Maybe it was time to take a break. Mom had given him some money, and he felt sure he could persuade Rose to stop skiing and go and buy some candy.

But, tired or not, Rose wasn't slowing down much. Eric knew from hard experience how important timing was with his sister—too early and she would dig in her heels and refuse to do what he was suggesting, too late and there would be tears before he had a chance to suggest anything. Maybe he should let her have a couple more runs.

As he watched the snowy scene before him, Eric's mind drifted back to the late Cretaceous. Despite all the time he had spent there, he still had lots of unanswered questions. What was causing the colder climate? What had introduced the sickness? What was the significance of these factors in the end of Weet's world? Most importantly, what was going to happen to the relationship he had seen developing between Weet and Saar? After the first visit, Eric had been in a turmoil of uncertainty and anticipation. He had wanted desperately to go back and see Weet again. This had partly been because Rose remembered nothing of their adventure and partly because of the loneliness that Eric felt back in this world. He had been confident that if he could only return to Weet's world, the loneliness would vanish when he was back with his new friend. But it had not turned out that way. The look in Weet's eyes when he had first seen Saar had told Eric that his friendship with Weet could never be the same from that moment on. He still wanted to go back, his curiosity was too strong not to, but this time the loneliness was there, not here.

Rose remembered the second adventure, and they could share memories of all the wonderful things that had happened. Eric had not mentioned their adventures to Gran, even though she still seemed to be the one adult who would understand and not dismiss his stories as wild imaginings. Now that Rose remembered, it didn't seem so necessary to have an adult understand.

What *was* necessary was to find an answer to all his questions. He had read all the books. Eric smiled to himself. All those arguments he had read in books! They were a waste of time. Eric had experienced more than the authors ever would; he had felt the warm Cretaceous air, had seen the sick hadrosaurs and the disease-carrying bugs; he had even felt the warmth of a dinosaur's body as he had ridden on its back and seen the sky fill with trails of fire as pieces of rock hurtled through the atmosphere. But what did it all mean? Eric desperately wanted to know.

A scream shook Eric out of his reverie. He was

almost expecting to see a tyrannosaurus strolling across the slopes, but he saw Rose instead. She had snuck across and up the steeper slopes while Eric was lost in thought, and now she was hurtling down. Normally, she would have been all right, but she was tired and completely out of control. Without a second thought, Eric pushed off from the tree and headed for his flying sister.

Eric angled across the slope, aiming for a point where he could intercept her. What he would do when they both got there wasn't clear, but he had to do something. Rose was wobbling all over the place, waving her arms about. Miraculously, she hadn't fallen yet, but that only meant she was going faster. There was a very real danger that she would injure herself, or someone else. If Eric could reach her, perhaps he could ski alongside her and slow her down before she hit something.

Rose was very close now and still screaming. He ducked to avoid a flying ski pole and reached over to grab at Rose's jacket, but it didn't work. Eric had forgotten Sally. As he slowed down, the dog, excited by all this activity after such a dull morning and free from her loosened collar, shot past him, straight into Rose's legs. Rose fell against Eric. Eric swerved to the left as they both fell, right at a large spruce tree. He only had time to throw himself to the snow before the tangled mass of skis, people and dog crashed into the heavy trunk.

Eric's head cracked against the hard wood. His world exploded into a thousand spots of coloured light and pain. His last conscious impression was of floating down a long black tunnel towards a faint light far in the distance.

CHAPTER 3

another beach

Weet strode easily along the beach. The gravel crunched under his feet and rolled noisily about under the incoming waves. Above him, wheeling birds filled the air with their raucous cries. At his side, Sinor skipped playfully along. Already the blood-red sun was settling on the horizon. Soon the hazy air would catch fire in the sunset, and the chill of night would settle over the island. Weet glanced up uneasily, but it was too early. The sky was still too bright for him to pick out the strange streaks of fire which had been growing larger and brighter over the past weeks.

It had been a successful day. Over his shoulder Weet carried a long sharpened stick, on which were impaled three large fish. The bag hanging at his waist was filled with shellfish. There was more than enough for a good supper for them all. But Weet was not happy.

It had been a year since the velociraptor attack on the tree city and the meteor storm, and, on the surface, things seemed to be going quite well. The survivors had created a thriving community on the island, taking everything they needed from the forest or the surrounding sea. Weet's ability to make fire helped during the increasingly cold nights. The roaring blaze in the middle of the sleeping circle had given them a sense of security and comfort after the terrors of the year before. There had been a lot of discussion around the fire about the possibility of heading back over Fire Mountain to Weet's home, but once they had learned how to use the resources around them, life had settled into a comfortable routine, and there had seemed less and less reason to undertake such a perilous journey.

Weet was sure that, had he been alone, he would have attempted it. This wasn't his home, and he missed his family and the familiar life beside the inland sea, but there was Saar. She had wanted to remain on the island, and Weet had not been prepared to leave her. So he had stayed and settled, but his mind was still restless. He often thought about Eric, Rose and Sally. They had visited his world twice now, and he regarded them as his friends.

Weet thought back to the first time he had met the three. They had been so odd and helpless. If Weet hadn't arrived when he had, they would have shortly been a velociraptor's dinner. They had certainly learned a lot in their time in Weet's world, but Weet had changed too. Then, he had been little more than a hatchling and so much, even in his own world, had been new and puzzling. Now he was an adult. He had undertaken a quest in search of his past, found another world whose existence he had not even suspected and fallen in love.

But Eric, Rose and Sally would always be special to him. They had gone through so much together: saved each other's lives, faced down Tyrannosaurus rex, braved the terrors of Fire Mountain. He had learned much from them, especially since he had picked up their odd, guttural language, but he still had a feeling that there was more to learn. Their connection to his world was strong, but there was no way of knowing when, or if, they would return. Last time, he had waited three years before they had come back, and now another year had passed. He was reminded of something else. The fire nights were due again. This time, would they simply be streaks of fire in the sky as they had been in the past, or would there be another storm of terror and chaos, like a year ago? Weet found himself glancing anxiously at the sky as he walked.

A large green crab, startled by Sinor, rose from a clump of seaweed and scuttled down the shingle on its spindly legs. Weet ignored it, since there was not enough meat in the legs or body to make the risk of a nasty nip from the large pincers worthwhile. Sinor followed at a respectable distance until the crab disappeared into the surf, then returned to Weet's heels.

Weet was travelling slowly now. It had been a long day, and he was tired. It was hard work trying to catch food that ran around, hid and, when caught, often bit. Weet reflected that it was much easier to just eat things that grew on bushes and waited for you to pick them. He still hadn't developed much of a taste for the food here. Some of the fish wasn't too bad if it was cooked over the fire long enough, but Weet had never developed a taste for the shells that Saar took straight from the rocks, broke open, and ate raw with such obvious relish.

The worst thing had been the long-necked creature the survivors had managed to kill when it had dragged its cumbersome body ashore to lay its eggs. Weet hadn't been there, but the fight had apparently been epic, with the creature darting its head around on the end of a long neck as the hunters tried to slip in and cut its throat without being impaled on its rows of razor-sharp teeth. Their return with huge sides of blubbery meat had been met with great excitement. Weet had been less than enthusiastic about the fat-dripping hunks of half-raw flesh he was offered. He had eaten some, but he hoped it would be a long time before the brave hunters found another creature like that.

Weet turned off the beach and headed into the trees. The path through the woods was quicker, and it gave him a chance to pick some fruit. The fruit on the island wasn't nearly as good as the delicious apps and nans he remembered from home. It was smaller and had much less flavour, but it was better than slimy raw shellfish or greasy blubber.

Even though there were no velociraptors on the island, the trees closing in around him still made Weet nervous. He preferred open spaces where he didn't feel that something could creep up on him. He had only been back to the mainland once in the last year, and he hadn't seen any velociraptors there either, but that didn't mean there weren't still some hiding somewhere. The tree city was deserted and derelict. Already the platforms were beginning to rot, and creepers were growing over the stalls in the market. Despite his unpleasant experiences there, Weet felt sad. The city had been the people's way of adapting to the velociraptor threat, just as travelling over the mountains had been his ancestors'. Sometimes it seemed to Weet that he was destined to lose everything he valued, his home and family, the tree city, Eric, Rose and Sally. All he had left were Saar and Sinor.

The memory of his friends from the other world added to his sadness. He missed them. He had told Saar all about their adventures and even attempted to teach her some of the children's strange language, but she had not been very interested. Saar had never had a chance to get to know them properly and was a very practical person by nature, content to focus on immediate needs. In fact, the comfortable life they now led on the island was largely the result of her drive.

Weet smiled. Despite it all, he was more or less happy here with Saar and the survivors. If only he could get rid of this yearning to go home.

"Help!" Weet's smile broadened. That was a word from Eric's language, just the way he used to speak it.

"Help! Help! Help!" And that was Rose! It wasn't his imagination! There was Sally's familiar bark.

Weet dropped his fish and pushed his way through the undergrowth in the direction of his friends' cries.

CHAPTER 4

return

As his memory returned, a frightening thought swam into Eric's consciousness.

"Avalanche!"

He had been skiing over to save Rose. An avalanche must have knocked them down and buried them alive.

No, that wasn't right. His ski boots felt heavy and awkward, but he could move them. The only avalanche he had encountered had been small and furry. Then the spruce tree floated back into his memory. He could still feel its trunk against his back. The severe pain in the back of his head gave him the feeling that if he moved too fast, it would split open, and his tired brains would spill out onto the snow.

Snow? Eric's hand was lying by his side. His ski glove was missing and he could feel the ground. It was soft like snow, but it was warm, and when he curled his fingers, they dug into unmistakable earth. And it really was becoming uncomfortably hot. Eric opened his eyes gently. There were trees all around him. He must be farther into the woods than he thought. Sally was beside him looking around dazedly, and Rose was draped over Eric's outstretched legs. She wasn't moving.

Eric leaned forward gingerly. The pain in his head was excruciating, and he was beginning to sweat uncomfortably. Lightly, he shook Rose's shoulder. His sister groaned.

"Leave me alone," she mumbled. "I don't want to go to school today. I think I've got a fever."

"No, you don't," said Eric, "and it's not a school day. We're on holiday, and you had a skiing accident."

"No, I didn't." Rose opened her eyes and struggled to sit up. "I was doing fine until you tripped me."

Now it was Eric's turn to groan. Rose had the most annoying habit of changing the past to suit how she felt.

"Where are we?" she exclaimed. "This isn't the ski slope. There's no snow."

"I don't know." Eric shook his head and immediately regretted it as waves of pain washed over him. If only his head didn't hurt so much, then he might be able to concentrate. "Maybe the trees have sheltered us. Help should be here by now. Even if we've only been unconscious for a few minutes, someone should have come. Let's shout so they know where we are."

"Help!" he called as loudly as he could. Rose looked at her brother pityingly.

"Help! Help! Help!" she shouted in a high-pitched almost-scream. Excited by the noise, Sally joined in with a series of barks.

"That should do it," Rose remarked. "But something's not right." She looked puzzled.

"Yes," Eric agreed. He had a strong feeling that something was wrong, but he couldn't grasp what it was. He felt confused and wished his head didn't hurt so badly. Still, their shouting had worked, someone was coming. The bushes in front of him were rustling.

It took Eric a moment to realize what was going on. He had been expecting ski patrol in orange, but instead there was a tall, thin green figure standing in the dappled sunlight.

"Weet!" Rose was on her ski-booted feet and stumbling awkwardly towards the figure, with Sally close behind.

"Of course," thought Eric dully, "Weet—time travel—we're back." He struggled to stand and join his sister and Sally, but the effort was too much. A wave of nausea swept over him, and his vision blurred. Then everything went black as he slumped back to the ground at the foot of the tree.

Weet's heart was pounding by the time he reached his friends, and his mind was in turmoil. They were back! They would laugh together again and share adventures. And perhaps Weet would finally discover the answers to the mysteries he was sure Eric knew.

Weet pushed the last branch aside and stopped. There were his three friends all right—but they had changed. They were all puffed up and had strange things on their feet. Even when Rose called his name and stood up, she could hardly run. Only Sally looked the same as she bounded forward. Then Rose was on him, throwing her arms around his waist and shouting, "Weet! Weet! We're back! It's so good to see you again."

Weet hugged his small friend in return and reached to scratch Sally's ear as she bounded around with Sinor at his feet. He was stopped by the sight of Eric falling back to the ground. Disengaging himself, he hurried over to the foot of the tree. Eric was slumped against the trunk with his eyes closed. He was breathing, but his face was red and there was water running out of it. His body was bright purple and all puffed up.

Rose arrived and crouched beside Weet. Sally began licking Eric's outstretched hand and Sinor sat to the side, head cocked inquisitively.

"He hit his head," said Rose. "He looks hot. Let's get him out of his snow suit."

Weet didn't know what Rose was talking about, but he helped as much as he could as she removed his strange boots and unzipped the suit that made him look so puffed up. Beneath it, Eric looked more normal in the second skins Weet recognized from before. Rose repeated the process on herself.

"That feels better," she commented. "I think he's coming round."

Eric was beginning to move and was letting out some low groans.

"Come on," encouraged Rose, mopping his face with the sleeve of her shirt, "we're back and Weet's here."

Eric opened his eyes and said "Weet" weakly. He looked around at his companions but appeared to have trouble focusing.

"Dark soon," Weet responded, glancing up at the sky through the trees. "We go fire?" He didn't want to be caught in the woods in the darkness. It was safe enough, there were no large predators on the island; nevertheless, the dark made Weet uncomfortable and, if Eric was sick, he would be better able to tend to him at the camp.

"You walk?" Weet asked. Eric nodded and immediately closed his eyes again in pain. Gingerly,

supported on either side by Weet and Rose, Eric got to his feet.

"Skins?" asked Weet, nodding back at the crumpled piles of ski clothing and boots.

"I don't think we'll need them here," Rose answered, "and we can pick them up tomorrow if we want."

Helping support Eric, they made their way back to where Weet had left his fish. Fortunately, the ground was soft, and Eric and Rose's winter socks were enough to protect them from the prickly carpet of pine needles.

As they walked, Weet's mind was full of conflicting emotions. He was happy at the return of his friends, but he was worried about Eric. He hoped that Eric and Rose would be able to finally answer some of his questions, but he was strangely nervous about what those answers might be.

And there was something else. How would their return affect the relationship he had built with Saar? As long as Weet had only imagined his friends' return, there was no conflict. Now that they were here, Weet felt torn.

What if the three most important people in his life wanted different things from him? How would he decide? Still, that was in the future. For the moment, all that mattered was getting Eric back to the camp.

CHAPTER 5
some questions answered

Weet's arrival with Eric, Rose, and Sally caused quite a stir among the island residents. Even those who had seen the trio a year before in the tree city were disturbed by their sudden reappearance. Weet could do little to explain where they had come from. To his great relief, both Soron and Saar accepted his friends with few questions.

In the last year, a thriving little community had grown up on the island. It was defined on one side by a line of boats drawn up on the beach, and on the other by the forest. Between, a large area had been cleared of trees and underbrush and was now dotted with an assortment of huts and shelters. A few of the refugees had opted for a more isolated life and had built dwellings farther into the trees. Some had even built tree houses in imitation of the tree city, but the open area by the beach was the acknowledged centre of the community.

It was here that Weet brought the stunned Eric and

his companions. The sun had finally disappeared, and the darkness was gathering around them as they sat on a circle of logs around a fire pit and were offered fruit and fish. Eric, who had been only vaguely aware of the journey here, began to brighten as he rested and ate some apps. Saar applied some damp leaves to the lump on the back of his head. The leaves felt cool and soothing and eased the pain. Rose fussed around him like a mother hen.

"It's okay, Rose," Eric said at last. "I'm fine. Sit down and have some fruit."

"Well, if you don't want my help," Rose replied, sitting down and biting into a nan.

"Yecch, it's sour." Weet said, reminding them of the first time they had tried the fruit of his world. Eric and Rose laughed at the memory as he joined them.

"He"o, Eric," he said as he sat down.

"Hello, Weet," said Eric, smiling at the familiar figure. "Still having trouble with the "l" sound, I see."

Weet nodded. "I practice," he said. Then, after a pause, "I happy you back."

"I'm glad to be back too," said Eric and Rose in unison.

"How long have we been away?" Eric added.

"One year since fire night."

Eric shivered at the memory.

"Has the fire night come again?" he asked. Weet shook his head.

A bright flash made Eric look up. It was just a shooting star, and it wasn't what made him gasp as he looked at the darkening sky. His gasp made Rose's head snap back too. The sky was dark enough to see the stars clearly. They looked just as foreign and mysterious as they had on the previous visits, and several more shooting stars flashed across their field of view as they watched, but that wasn't what was upsetting him. Across the highest point of the sky was a string of shining lights. They were fuzzy and varied in size, but even the smallest was easily much brighter than the brightest star. Eric guessed that there were at least twenty of them, and each had a short tail. They were like a necklace of silver commas strung up in the heavens.

"What are they?" asked Rose breathlessly.

"Comets," replied Eric quietly, "or at least bits of comets."

"They're beautiful," Rose said.

Eric agreed. They were beautiful, but the sight of them had sent an icy shiver down his spine. They were also deadly. It might have been a comet which had—would—destroy the dinosaurs' world. Weet's world. As Eric gazed upward, he remembered the pictures he had seen on the internet of comet fragments which had slammed into Jupiter a few years before. They had caused unimaginable havoc, and each had been large enough to have destroyed much of the life on Earth, if it had been their target. As his eyes scanned the long, beautiful line, they rested on the fifth one from the right. It wasn't the brightest, but there was something about it. . .

"Polar Bears," he muttered under his breath.

"What?" asked Rose, her eyes still fixed on the sky. "What do Polar Bears have to do with anything?"

"I'm not sure," Eric was speaking slowly as a thought formed in his mind. "I remember reading somewhere that when you see a Polar Bear in the Arctic, the time to be scared is if it doesn't appear to be moving. That means it's heading straight for you."

"So?" Rose's neck was beginning to hurt, but she couldn't take her eyes off the sky.

"Well, look at the fifth spot on the right. Notice anything different about it?"

"Tell me, Eric. I don't want to play games."

"It's the only one that doesn't have a tail."

It was true. Rose could see that all the other bright spots had tails. Some were longer than others, and one even appeared to have two tails, but the fifth one from the right was the only one with no sign of a tail at all.

"What does that mean?" Rose asked.

"I'm not sure," replied her brother. "It might be

that it's made of different stuff, but it might mean that it has a tail and we can't see it because it's coming straight towards us."

Rose was silent for a moment. Then she lowered her head and rubbed her stiff neck. "Is that the one that's going to hit Mexico?" she asked.

"Maybe," Eric replied. He glanced across at Weet, who was watching his friends intently. How much did he understand? Mexico would mean nothing to him, it wouldn't even exist for 65 million years, but Weet wasn't dumb. He must know something was going on. On their last visit, Eric had come close to telling Weet what he knew about the fate of Weet's world. Only the meteorite storm had stopped him. Now he felt he owed it to Weet. He wished he had more time, but then sometimes thinking about things didn't do any good. It was better to just do it.

"Weet," he said, meeting his friend's gaze and speaking slowly, "there's something I have to tell you, and it's not good." Eric paused and took a deep breath. "In my time, way in the future," Eric waved his arms vaguely to try and indicate the future, "there are no roarers, or crestnecks, or shovelbills, or..." He couldn't say Weets. "Something happened. A comet or an asteroid." How much of this did Weet understand? "A huge rock"—Eric's arms were working again—"hit the Earth. It caused a lot of damage and made the weather different. All the plants died, there were fires and floods and earthquakes. Even the roarers and the others died. Only the marats survived. I don't know when this happened, but I think it might be soon."

But when was soon, tomorrow, or a million years down the road? The fire nights and the comets were scary, but the solar system was a big place. Rocks might spin around for decades before one hit the Earth. Eric stopped talking before he got too complicated. Rose was looking at Weet. The three sat in silence for a long time. Eric began to wonder if Weet had understood and was about to start again when he spoke.

"How know?" he asked. It took Eric a moment to understand the question.

"Oh," he said eventually, "how do I know all this?" Weet nodded. "Well, people have found the bones of crestnecks and the other animals that live now." Eric thought of the box of bone fragments under his bed in Calgary—not much left from a whole world. Weet interrupted his thought.

"Found Weet bones?" he asked.

The question dismayed Eric. "No," he said instinctively, before he remembered the three long, thin fingers he had discovered in the side of the hoodoo outside Drumheller. Maybe that wasn't Weet. "I don't think so," he added lamely.

Weet stared into the fire.

"Weet," Eric continued, "there is more." Weet didn't move, so Eric kept on. "Whether the big one hits soon or more fire nights come, this is a very dangerous place." That got Weet's attention. He looked up.

"There are a lot of pieces of rock flying about up there. If only a small one lands in the ocean, it could cause a wave which would wash right over the top of this island."

Weet gazed at Eric without speaking for a long time. At last he nodded slowly.

So this was the secret Eric had been carrying with him all this time. This was what Weet had longed to know ever since he had first met Eric cowering before the velociraptor attack. It was the answer he had gone on his quest to discover. All his actions in the four years since Eric, Rose and Sally had first arrived had been spent trying to find this knowledge. Weet's world was doomed. There was almost a strange sense of relief in finally knowing.

Weet glanced at the sky. Lines of bright light were continually flashing across the dark areas between the stars. It had been like this for nights now, almost as though the stars themselves were falling from the sky. His eye drifted to the chain of apparently immobile brighter lights. Was that the end of everything he knew coming towards him? It seemed inconceivable. Certainly there was danger in the sky, as the fire nights last year had proved, but mostly it seemed so constant and safe, a canopy of blue by day and stars by night, the same day after day—secure. Now Weet had been told that something which could destroy himself and all he knew and loved was going to come from the sky. It was hard to grasp. Nevertheless, Weet believed his friend. His world was changing, and he had long had a vague feeling that something was going to happen. Now he knew what it was.

Both Eric and Rose sat looking at Weet from across the fire, their odd rubbery faces stretched in almost comical expressions. He would have to tell Saar and the rest, if what Eric said about the danger to the island was true. Suddenly Weet made a decision. This was not where he belonged, and he had not been totally content in the last year. He had adjusted well to life here, but it was not his. If the end was coming, he wanted to be amongst familiar things, living in a tree circle, not on a beach; he wanted to eat decent fruit and to talk with his family. He fervently hoped he could persuade Saar to come with him but, come what may, Weet was going home.

After what seemed like an age to Eric, Weet stood up.

"Thank you," he said to Eric, before stepping out of the firelight and going over to Saar.

"Do you think he understands?" asked Rose.

"He understands," replied Eric. "He may not have understood all the words, but he knows what's going to happen. I guess he's telling Saar now. I wonder what he will do?"

"What'll *we* do?" As usual, Rose went right to the heart of the matter.

"I don't know." Eric gazed thoughtfully into the flickering flames. "Maybe this is why we came, to warn Weet. Maybe we'll go back now."

"I don't think so," interrupted Rose. "We've always stayed for a few days, and it wouldn't be fair to just leave Weet with this."

Eric chuckled. He had never thought that time travel should be fair. But he knew what Rose meant. It would be cruel to leave now. But what were they going to do? Did they have to stay to witness the end, or would they go back to their time after a few days of adventure?

"I don't think so either," replied Eric, "but I don't know what will happen. I guess we'll have to wait and see what Weet decides to do."

"What will happen if number five is the one and it hits while we're still here?" Rose turned her eyes skyward.

Eric shrugged. "I don't really know. No one has ever seen a large impact on the Earth. All the stuff I've read was guesswork. It depends on so many things: what angle it hits at, whether it's a single piece, where it hits, and what it's made of. Comets are mostly ice and dirt, and meteorites are either stony or iron. All those things make a big difference. We do know that the one 65 million years before our time landed in the ocean and dug a hole all the way through the Earth's crust. But exactly what happened after that is speculation. Some people think planet-wide fires killed everything, others that it was the dust cloud causing the climate to change... or the earthquakes, or even strong acid rain. So no one knows for sure. Scientists can make computers paint nice pictures of what might have happened, but whether they're true or not depends on what information they put in in the first place, and we don't know everything."

"Would everything be killed all at once?"

Eric shivered. That wasn't a question he really wanted to think about.

"Probably not. The shock wave and fireball would kill all life within hundreds of kilometres. The rest of the world would have earthquakes, tidal waves, and continent-wide fires. Some people think the tidal waves were big enough to wash over North America. All the dust thrown up would probably cover the earth and block all the sunlight. About three-quarters of all species on Earth died out, but for some it might have taken months or even years. No one knows."

Eric lapsed into silence. Rose's curiosity seemed satisfied for the moment. Eric glanced at Weet, who was still deep in conversation with Saar. A wave of loneliness swept over the boy. He had often thought about telling Weet what was going to happen to his world, and he had imagined many scenarios, but all had involved Weet and himself talking about what they would do and what it meant. In reality, he had simply been a messenger carrying information which Weet could use to decide what he would do with his life—a life that now included Saar and seemed to exclude Eric. He felt his eyes fill with tears. He was tired, and after all, his head was still sore. Eric slid to the ground so that he could rest his back against the log. The fire was warm and comforting, but the tears wouldn't stop. Rose slid down beside her brother, put an arm around him and nestled her head into his shoulder.

"It's okay," she whispered. Eric nodded mutely. Not wanting to be left out, Sally wandered over and pushed between the two children. After some wriggling, she got herself comfortable and, by the time Weet returned to the fire, all three were fast asleep.

Weet and Saar sat together by the roaring fire. Weet had just finished explaining what he understood of what Eric had just told him. Saar gazed into the flames in silence. At last, she looked up.

"The whole world will end?" she whistled.

The tone of her voice carried such sadness that Weet felt a lump come into his throat. Maybe he shouldn't have told her. Maybe it was better not to know.

"It might not happen for years," he added lamely.

"But it might happen tomorrow," Saar said, "and the Fire Nights are due."

Weet nodded slowly.

Saar sighed. Then she came to a decision. She took a deep breath and squared her shoulders.

"Well," she said firmly, "then we must go. First to higher ground. If Eric is right, this place is dangerous. We must move the people to the hills."

Weet could only nod once more. The strength of her statements overwhelmed him. Saar's wide eyes gazed straight into Weet's.

"And you must go," she added.

WILSON

"What?" Weet was stunned.

"Yes," Saar continued, "you must go, past Fire Mountain to warn your people. They must know too and do what they can to prepare."

Weet suddenly felt left behind—swamped by Saar's decisiveness.

"I will go," he said quietly. "But alone, I am only half. Will you come with me?"

For what seemed like an eternity, Saar stared into Weet's eyes. Weet felt as if his entire future were hanging in the balance. He had to go, and he would be glad of Eric, Rose and Sally's company, but without Saar he would be empty. Surely, the purpose of his quest had been to lead him to Saar. He couldn't lose her now.

Eventually, Saar blinked.

"I will come," she said quietly.

Despite the unknown horrors facing him, Weet felt a rush of joy at the news. He put his arms around Saar, and together they sat in silence by the fire.

CHAPTER 6

island living

Eric awoke without the faintest idea where he was. He was lying on a mat of twigs, and sunlight was dappling through a rough roof of branches over his his head. His mouth was dry, and he had a dull headache. Fragmentary images of skiing, forests and shooting stars swirled in his befuddled brain.

"Come on, sleepyhead! It's time to get up." Rose's cheerful face appeared in the entrance to Eric's rough shelter. She was carrying fruit, which she pushed in beside her brother. Eric sat up groggily.

"How did we get here?" he asked slowly.

"Weet carried us over after we fell asleep by the fire last night," Rose replied. "I don't remember a thing about it. We must have slept for ages. It was light when I got up, and that was more than an hour ago. How's your head?"

"Better." Rose's happy babble was comforting, and gave Eric a chance to collect his thoughts.

"Where's Weet?"

"He's down on the beach, getting ready to leave. I think. . . "

"Leave?" Eric interrupted. "Why leave? Where is he going?"

"I think he's going home. There was. . . "

"Home? Why is he going home?"

"Eric!" Rose exclaimed in exasperation. "If you would stop interrupting, I could tell you." She folded her arms across her chest and glared at him.

"Sorry," he said. "Please go on."

Mollified, Rose continued. "There was a meeting last night. I'm not sure what went on, but Weet and a few others are loading a couple of boats. When I asked him what was happening, all he said was 'Home! Home!' and pointed over to the mainland."

Picking up a couple of pieces of fruit, Eric crawled out of the lean-to and stood up. Their ski suits and boots were neatly laid out on the sand. He didn't think they would need them.

"Let's go see what's going on," he said.

They headed across the clearing for the beach, Eric chewing on the fruit and Rose chattering happily to him. The beach was just as Eric remembered it, but it still took his breath away. The tide was out, and a vast expanse of almost white sand stretched down to the distant line of surf. The water was almost unimaginably blue, and the air was filled with a variety of flying creatures. As Eric watched, a strange beast, about twice the size of an eagle, swept into view. It was flying parallel to the shore, skimming the water's surface. It was propelled by stately flaps of its broad, furry wings and steered with a flat, oval rudder set on the end of a long tail. Almost a third of its total length was head, and most of that was an odd beak, curved upwards like the hull of a boat and lined with rows of very fine, needle-like teeth. Every few wing-beats, the creature would dip its head to carve a furrow in the still water with its beak. Eric was sure he could see small creatures wriggling helplessly on the teeth every time the head was raised.

"A pterosaur," he said breathlessly. "To think people used to say that they could only glide. That one's flying as well as any bird I've ever seen."

As the pterosaur disappeared along the beach, Eric's eye was drawn to a scene much closer. Among a riot of driftwood discarded by the last high tide, Eric could see Weet and five others. They were gathered round two boats. Saar was there, and so was her father Soron, the old shell-seller. They were busy packing supplies into the boats. Sally and Sinor were playing in the sand, but stopped their game when they spotted the children and ran to frolic at their feet. Weet looked up as they approached.

"S'eep good?" he asked.

"Yes, thank you," replied Eric, "and thanks for carrying us to bed."

Weet nodded. "How head?" he said, pointing at Eric.

"Better," the boy replied, touching the large bump beneath his hair. "What's going on?" he asked, pointing at the boats.

Weet hesitated. He indicated a large log nearby and turned to whistle at the group of people, who had stopped work to watch. Saar put down a bag she was holding and came over. The group sat down on the log.

"I go home," Weet began. "Saar too." Weet's mind skipped back to his conversation with Saar the night before.

After the children had fallen asleep, he and Saar had called a meeting. They had agreed not to mention the possible destruction of their world, but Weet had talked about the danger to the island from tidal waves. There were a lot of worried questions, but things hadn't settled down until Soron took charge. He seemed to understand that there was more to all this than Weet and Saar were saying. He had talked of organizing an exodus back to the mainland and establishing a community on higher ground. The people had calmed down, because

Soron was very well-respected, and he had presented the idea very positively. It was to be a spiritual return to the old way of life. The meeting had broken up into small groups discussing ways to make the journey. Weet and Saar had confided the whole story to Soron, and then had gone to begin preparations for their long journey.

"You come too?" Weet asked Eric, as he returned to the present.

Eric looked at Rose. "Sure," he said, when she nodded. "Of course we'll come. It's our adventure too."

"Good," responded Weet, standing up. "We go when sun high." He waved his arm above his head and, with Saar beside him, set off back to the boats.

"Well," said Rose, gazing at the retreating backs, "here we go again."

"Yeah," agreed Eric. Then a thought struck him. "What do we do with our snowsuits and boots?"

"Leave them," said Rose without hesitation. "We'll never wear them, and I don't want to carry mine past Fire Mountain."

"Okay, but your sweatshirt didn't come back with us last time, and I would hate to lose my ski stuff. Mom would be furious."

"If we're going to get hit by a big lump of rock from outer space, my snowsuit won't help. You carry yours if you want, but I'm leaving mine." Rose turned her back on Eric and marched over to help load the boats.

"One thing about my sister," he said to Sally, who was looking up at him, "when she makes her mind up, it stays made up." Then he went to help pack bags of food for the journey.

CHAPTER 7

going back

Eric and Rose soon realized that their attempts to help were more of a hindrance. Everyone seemed to know exactly what they were doing and where everything should go. After a while Eric turned to Rose. "Come on," he said, "we're just in the way. It's going to be a while before things are ready. Let's go for a walk."

The pair walked along the beach in silence. The sand was warm and comfortable on their bare feet. Occasionally, Eric bent down to pick up an interesting shell or rock. At length, they reached the rocky promontory that marked the corner of the island and separated the sandy beach from the pebbly one Weet had walked along the evening before. Climbing the smooth rock, they found a comfortable spot where the rock dropped off into fairly deep water. Peering into the depths, Eric could see small fishes darting about. They looked no different from fish he had seen at the coast or in the Vancouver

Aquarium. Eventually Rose broke the long silence.

"It's beautiful," she said.

"Yes," agreed Eric. "In a way I'll be sorry to leave. I'm not looking forward to the journey past Fire Mountain—especially without shoes."

Rose nodded and looked down at her feet, which were already looking extremely grubby. "As far as I can remember from the trip out here, the ground was pretty soft, but then we were on the back of Weet's dinosaur most of the time."

"The maiasaura," said Eric thoughtfully, gazing at the distant horizon, "poor thing."

"Look!" said Rose, interrupting his reminiscences. Eric looked up.

"Yes, I see it."

It was a long streak of fire stretching in an almost leisurely way across the sky.

"Is it the big one?" Rose sounded nervous.

"No," Eric reassured her. "It's too small and heading north."

They watched for several long seconds until the object passed below the dark shapes of the mainland hills.

"Will it land somewhere?" Rose asked softly.

"I don't know. Some meteorites just skim the atmosphere and shoot off into space again. Whatever happens to that one, the sky seems a lot more active than when we were last here. The comets and all the shooting stars last night are making me nervous." He paused for a moment, then, turning back to Rose, continued: "Do you think I did the right thing telling Weet that his world was doomed?"

"Uh-huh," Rose grunted in response, "keeping the secret was really bothering you."

"True," Eric agreed, "and Weet did seem to take it well. It was almost as if he wanted an excuse to go back. Still, I wonder. . . " Eric stopped speaking and his jaw fell open. His gaze had wandered away from Rose, and now it was fixed on something over her left shoulder.

"What. . . ?" was all Rose managed before Eric's urgent, whispered "Ssh!" silenced her. "Turn your head very slowly and look over your shoulder."

Rose did as she was told. What she saw made her gasp. A creature was pulling itself out of the water onto a sloping shelf of rock only ten or twelve metres away. It was about two metres long, and at least half of it was a sinuous neck. The body was mottled dark greenish-brown on top and light grey underneath. It was struggling almost comically to pull itself onto the rock with its stiff front flippers. The small head on the end of the neck was waving around all over the place.

"It's a baby elasmosaur," whispered Eric, "like

the one we saw in the museum at Courtenay on Vancouver Island."

Rose nodded slowly. "It's so cute."

"The guy at the museum said he wondered if they came out of the water to breed. I guess we know now."

The elasmosaur was concentrating so hard on climbing that it was completely oblivious of its audience. Despite its awkward progress, its entire length was now well clear of the water. As the pair watched, an uncomfortable thought began to form in Eric's mind. However, Rose put it into words first.

"Isn't it kind of young to be on its own?"

Eric only had time to mumble "Yeah," before the deep water beside them erupted and a dripping head appeared. It was the same as the one on the baby behind them, but much larger. Two rows of needle-sharp teeth protruded from the jaws and formed a cage around the mouth. The head rose until it hung suspended above the two terrified children. "Don't move," whispered Eric out of the side of his mouth. He doubted whether the elasmosaur would be interested in eating them, but the teeth could do a lot of damage if it perceived them as a threat to its baby.

The head swung back and forth, examining the promontory for any threats. Water dripped off it, splashing Eric and Rose as the head swung in front of them, and the eye regarded them coldly. All at once, the mouth opened and the creature let out a loud barking cough. Rose jumped. It turned to look at her.

"Run!" screamed Eric, scrambling to his feet. His sudden movement startled the creature, and the head withdrew, but only momentarily. Eric and Rose had made six running steps before the head returned. It swept across the rock in a long graceful curve, catching Eric behind the shoulder and knocking him into Rose. The pair tumbled off the rock onto the sand where they lay in a heap. Sheltered by the bulk of the rock, Eric watched as the creature made a few more sweeps before retreating to collect its young and find a less bothersome place for sunbathing. When they were sure it had left, the pair disentangled themselves.

"Maybe I'm not so keen on staying here," said Eric weakly, as he brushed sand off himself. "Are you okay?"

"Yeah," said Rose looking up. "Oh Eric! You're bleeding."

Sure enough, a long scratch on his arm was trickling blood. As soon as he noticed it, it began to sting.

"Must have been one of the teeth when it bumped me," he said, wiping at the blood. "It's not deep, I'll live. Let's get back to Weet."

With much less spring in their steps, the pair made their way back along the beach.

The final farewells took longer than anticipated, and the tide was already retreating before they launched the two boats. Only Eric, Rose, Weet, Saar, Sinor and Sally were making the trip, but several survivors were accompanying them as far as the mainland, some to return the boats and others to follow and scout out a possible village sight on higher ground. The entire community lined the beach, waving a farewell to the party as they paddled away.

The voyage was uneventful, even though Eric couldn't help glancing over the side and thinking of the creatures lurking below. They paddled up the river, past the overgrown tree city which the survivors had abandoned a year ago on the night of the velociraptor attack. They camped for the night at the foot of the escarpment. Eric lay sleepless, watching the fireworks display in the night sky. Things seemed to be happening very fast all of a sudden. Somehow, ever since he had told Weet what was going to happen, he had lost control. He felt he was just being swept along by events. Perhaps that was the way it should be. After all, this was Weet's world, not his. But this was only day two of their visit, and already they had abandoned the island and set off on another journey. His eyes focused on the line of shining comets. Were they larger? Coming closer? He was still wondering when he finally dropped off to sleep.

The next morning, at the top of the escarpment, they said good-bye to the islanders, who spread out to search for a suitable site for the new community. Now they were on their own. All four had woven backpacks which hung comfortably from their shoulders. Weet's was full of assorted fruit and dried fish. Saar also had some food, but also many different kinds of medicinal leaves, each tied in its own bundle. Both Eric and Rose had food, but the children were surprised to find their ski clothes and even their boots stuffed carefully at the bottom. Rose wanted to dump them, but Eric thought that they might insult Weet by doing so. They compromised by hiding their heavy ski boots in some bushes and keeping the snowsuits. The suits were light and would make comfortable pillows at night.

It took the small party five days to reach Fire Mountain. The walking was easy, but Eric and Rose missed the maiasaura. Their bare feet hurt the first day, but that evening Saar rubbed some dark green leaves on their soles. The leaves produced a strong-smelling whitish juice, which stung at first, but soon eased the pain. By the end of day five and numerous rubbings of the leaves, both of the children's feet had toughened so much that they only noticed the sharpest stones.

Saar was the doctor for the group and could produce a leaf for almost any ailment. She seemed quite shy of the children, but was always helpful. Despite their inability to communicate except through Weet, Eric felt he was getting to know Saar better. Some of his resentment at the attention Weet paid to her disappeared in the face of her gentleness and kindness.

Weet was happy with the progress they were making. It was good to be on the move, and every step towards home was a thrill that not even the thought of Fire Mountain could quell. He was proud of Saar. He knew how worried she was at the thought of passing the volcanic peak. Weet was convinced that she believed him when he said there was a world on the other side of the mountain, but still, the stories from her childhood were powerful, and to go against them took a lot of courage. She had left behind her people, her past, everything she knew—

for what? An uncertain future far from her home.

On the morning of the seventh day since leaving the island they crested a ridge and saw the pumice desert stretching in endless grey before them. Fire Mountain loomed in the distance. Both Weet and Eric breathed a sigh of relief. The mountain was quiet, and only a narrow plume of smoke rose from the crater into the still air. There was no sign of the violent, belching cloud of ash they had encountered the time before. Eric laughed out loud at the sight.

"It's quiet," he said triumphantly.

"Yes," Weet agreed. This was going to be easy. He turned to Saar to share his pleasure, and his heart almost stopped.

She stood transfixed by the view. Her eyes were wide and her mouth hung open. This was the end of the world. Never mind what Weet said, she had never seen anything like this. Fire Mountain was huge and smoking. How could a mountain be on fire?

It had been bad enough leaving her people on the escarpment, but there had always been the thought that if she turned around and went back, they would be there waiting for her, and she could resume her life with them. This was different. If she could summon the courage to somehow pass this horror, she would be in a different world. There was no way she could ever be brave enough to do it twice. Helplessly, she looked at Weet. He stepped over to her and put a comforting arm around her shoulder.

"It is all right," he said. "Fire Mountain is quiet this time."

Quiet! If this was quiet, what had it been like when they had passed by before? She looked over at Eric. He had stopped making that funny choking noise that seemed to indicate happiness and was watching her with his odd, rubbery face. She would have to confront her fears. There was no doubt about that. If her friends could do it, so could she. Taking a deep breath, Saar set off across the pumice desert.

The ground remained reassuringly quiet as they crossed the desert. The climb onto the ridge by the mountain was the hardest part of the journey, and they were glad to stop and set up camp on the far slope. That night they sat around a small fire. Saar had been silent and determined all day. Weet had not strayed more than a metre from her side since the first view of the mountain, but now they were past it. Weet let the excitement he felt escape.

"Three days home," he said, making downhill motions with his hands.

"Yes," said Eric, "it's all downhill from here. We

were lucky Fire Mountain was asleep. It was a lot easier than the last time we came this way."

Saar looked around at this strange world that she had been brought up to believe couldn't exist. Yet here she was in it. Relaxing, she nestled against Weet's shoulder.

"Welcome to my world," he whispered.

"Thank you," she replied. "It is my world now too. I look forward to you showing it to me."

"I will," said Weet. "I hope we can find my family. They would like to meet you."

"Isn't it cute?" Rose commented to Eric as their two friends sat with their heads almost touching, deep in conversation.

"Yeah," Eric replied, although inside he didn't think so. He and Weet had barely spoken on the journey. The feeling that he'd lost his friend was strong, and occasionally he had found himself wishing he were back in Vancouver or Calgary. At least there he would have decent shoes and not have to worry about being hit by a meteorite. In a way, he was bored. The days were monotonous.

WILSON

He had not seen any new animals since the encounter with the elasmosaur on the beach. Already this was their longest trip to the past, and Eric was certain that something would have to happen before they left. But what? He suspected that he knew. The comets were now definitely brighter and getting more so each night. The meteor shower was also getting stronger and, at times, had lit up the night as bright as day. All that heavenly activity was stressful and worried Eric. If the comet was going to hit, Eric almost wished it would do so and get it over with.

On the eighth day they passed the place where Eric, Rose and Sally had arrived the last time. The vegetation was larger and lusher than on the coastal side of Fire Mountain, but strangely, there were few large animals. They only spotted one herd of titanosaurs and several small lizards and birds. In the middle of the afternoon a large meteor blazed across the sky and disappeared to the north. It streaked across the line of comet fragments, which were now bright enough to be faintly visible in daylight. They travelled in silence for quite some time after they saw it, keeping their thoughts to themselves.

The ninth day was much the same. Saar continued to be fascinated by everything around her, and Weet continued to explain things to her.

That night, Eric lay watching the full moon. It was as huge as he remembered, outshining even the comet fragments. Despite its unfamiliar size, it still seemed friendly and reassuring. Eric found himself smiling slightly.

His smile vanished as a bright spot appeared on the right-hand edge of the yellow disk. In eerie silence, it blossomed into a large, reddish ball which stretched out into a long plume, eventually detaching itself from the moon's surface and fading into the vastness of space. Eric frowned. He knew what it was. Far above him an immense block of something, icy comet or solid rock, had smashed into the Earth's friendly old neighbour. With no atmosphere and little gravity, there had been nothing to prevent the results of the impact from being blown off into space. All that would be left would be one more lunar crater for astronomers to map millions of years down the road.

Eric shivered, closed his eyes, and drifted into sleep. That night his dreams were troubled by images of fiery collisions and horrible destruction. He awoke bleary-eyed and just as tired as he had been when he had gone to sleep.

On the tenth day the world ended.

CHAPTER 8

the last day

The last day of the Cretaceous Period began for the travellers much the same as those before it. They awoke, breakfasted on fruit, and set off downhill. Weet set the pace, keen to get back home. He could hardly contain his excitement at returning after a year away. He whistled constantly to Saar. Eric and Rose followed behind, chatting occasionally and enjoying the views. Sally and Sinor ranged far and wide between the bushes and trees on adventures only they could understand.

The landscape was as Eric remembered it, open grassland with low shrubs and clumps of large trees. The children's feet had toughened remarkably, which made walking easy on the gently rolling ground. Fruit was plentiful. Small, brightly-coloured birds darted between the bushes and set up a continual chirping background noise to any conversation. The sky was a soft, hazy blue and the high sun almost blotted out the string of silver comet fragments. It was almost possible to believe that all was well on such an idyllic morning. For the rest of his life, Eric would remember that morning as a perfect time, the last time he could imagine the world as simple and carefree.

Around midday, they crested a low hill and glimpsed their first view of the great inland sea. Below them, the land flattened out and the vegetation thickened towards the distant line of silver water. Eric could see rivers snaking on the last leg of their journey, and areas of swamp stood out as patches of deeper green. The tunnel through which he, Rose and Sally had first entered Weet's world was down there, as well as the tree ring where Weet's family had made their home. The maiasaura nesting site and the deserted hom village were also there, but there was danger too. Tyrannosaurus rex was there somewhere, as were the velociraptors, slower and more solitary than the ones on the coast, but no less deadly.

"Well, you're nearly home now," said Eric. Weet nodded as he gazed down. "How will you find your family?"

Weet turned to look at his friend.

"I go tree ring. If not, then at hatching. It soon." That seemed to make sense. Weet glanced over at Saar before continuing.

"We make tree ring," he said, gesturing at Saar. "You live us tree ring?"

The question took Eric aback. He hadn't thought what he would do when they arrived at Weet's old home. He had assumed that something was going to happen. But what if nothing did? What if this time, they stayed here for weeks, months, or even years? Already this was easily their longest visit, and there was no sign that it was about to end.

"I guess so. Thank you," Eric stuttered in response. He didn't really have any choice. Familiar as he and Rose were becoming with this world, they could hardly survive on their own.

"That would be lovely," added Rose cheerfully. "We'd be like one big family." Eric refrained from pointing out that Rose already had a family, 65 million years in the future. All of a sudden, he felt trapped in the middle, between his friend who had grown up and fallen in love, and his sister, who was still a child and unconcerned with life's complexities. Eric felt that he was neither. But he knew where he had to be.

"It will be lovely," he said, "but we will have to find our way back to our home."

He said this looking at Weet, who nodded slowly as Eric's meaning dawned on him. Rose was less easily convinced.

"Why?" she asked belligerently. "This is a beautiful place. It's always warmer than Calgary. The fruit is good—and no one has to go to school. When we do go back, we won't have lost any time in our world, so why not stay here as long as we can? I'd be happy living in a tree circle."

"What about T. rex?" Eric countered.

"Oh, there's not many of them, and we can keep out of their way. And Weet's whistling will keep the veloci-things away," she added, hurriedly anticipating her brother's next objection.

"Okay," he admitted, "this is a lovely place, and we could overcome the problems of living here. But it's not our place. I don't know why we've come here. I thought it might have been to warn Weet about what was going to happen, but we did that days ago and there's no sign of us going back. I don't know how long we'll be here, but we have to try and find our way home. That's where we belong."

Rose sat frowning, with her arms crossed defiantly across her chest.

"Well," she demanded in her most withering voice, "how are you going to get us home?"

"I don't know exactly," Eric had to admit, "but the tunnel that we came through the first time is the only place we've had any control over, and I'm sure I could find it again. If it's not too covered

WILSON

over, we might be able to get back in and crawl through."

"That's silly," said Rose immediately. "If we did that, we would arrive back in the badlands at Drumheller, when we came here from a ski slope at Whistler. How are we going to explain that to Mom and Dad? And anyway, what's to stop Weet and Saar following us through? What would we do with them? You couldn't hide them under your bed. They'd be trapped and taken to a zoo or something, and scientists would examine them forever. It would be a horrible life."

But it would be a life, Eric thought as he squinted up at the silver dots on either side of the sun. They seemed even brighter than yesterday.

"I don't know the answers," he said eventually. "I've never understood how or why these things are happening to us. It's just that I feel we should try to reach home if we can."

"Well, you can go if you want, and I'll stay here," said Rose huffily.

"No!" The loudness of Weet's voice took them both by surprise. He had been listening intently to them with his head cocked to one side. Now he gazed straight at Rose.

"Eric right," he said firmly. "I go home, you go home. Home where. . . " Weet paused, searching for the right words,". . . egg hatch," he continued.

Rose found herself smiling at the image, but Weet kept on: "Saar, me, new home. Rose, Eric, Sa"y, must find own home, grow up, and have eggs."

Eric and Rose burst out laughing at the notion. The tension evaporated.

"And when I do have eggs," said Rose through her laughter, "I'll call one of them Weet."

"Good," Weet said seriously. "We find you home."

Silence settled over the small group. Eric felt bad. He hadn't meant to get into a petty squabble. He felt like kicking himself. The way to get around Rose was not to meet her head-on. You had to talk your way around her. Now the special closeness they had sensed all morning was gone. The silence intruded into Eric's thoughts. He tilted his head and listened.

"The birds," he said at last, "the birds have stopped singing."

It was true. There was no birdsong, no rustling of small animals in the foliage, and no distant cry of frightened prey. A thick blanket of utter silence had descended on the world. It was eerie.

The four sat still. Even Sally and Sinor stopped their games and huddled motionless at their owners' feet. A moderately-sized meteor flashed low along the horizon over the inland sea. It disappeared in a bright flash, which was followed seconds later by a low, grumbling roar. Others followed, until the sky was alive with streaks of fire and continuous booming. Rose huddled with her hands over her ears. As abruptly as it had begun, the meteor storm ceased, but the silence didn't return. The sounds seemed to have startled the world back into activity. Birdsong erupted almost frantically all around. Sally threw back her head and let out an unearthly howl. Eric felt Rose shivering beside him.

"Is this the end?" she whispered.

"I don't know," replied Eric. "I don't think the big one was among that cluster—they all seemed to explode in the air."

"What's happening to the animals?" asked Rose.

"I don't know that either," Eric responded a little irritably. "Maybe the explosions scared them, or maybe there's an earthquake coming. Animals are supposed to act strangely before one."

As if to confirm his thought, about a dozen small shrew-like creatures burst from the bushes and ran past. They showed no awareness of the travellers, running across their outstretched legs as though they weren't there. Some larger creatures were thundering past on the other side of the hill. Eric looked up. The sky was filled with birds and pterosaurs of all shapes and sizes, heading north. It was as if all the birds and animals had simultaneously decided to migrate to the north pole.

"Where are they going?" Rose asked. "What's attracting them that way?"

"I don't know," said Eric, "Maybe something is scaring them." Eric looked south, towards the place he knew the big one was going to hit. But it obviously hadn't yet, so how did the animals know it was going to? Some sixth sense, like the one that warned them of coming earthquakes? Something strange was definitely about to happen. A horrible empty sense of doom was forming like a black knot in the pit of Eric's stomach.

"Do you think it's. . . ?"

"Maybe we should. . ."

Both Eric and Rose began to speak at the same moment, then stopped in confusion. Weet stood up.

"We go," he said.

"Yes," agreed Eric, "I think we should."

Hurriedly, the small group picked up their belongings. They were surrounded by the sounds of movement. Sally's howling had deteriorated to a low whine.

"Stop it, old girl," said Eric, bending to scratch her ear. "It's all right." But his comforting did little good. Sally quieted at his touch, but as soon as he removed his hand, she began whimpering again.

To Eric's surprise, Weet set off in the direction they had been heading for days.

"Wait!" Eric said, pointing north. "Shouldn't we

go that way, everything else is."

"No," replied Weet, turning towards Eric. "We go home." Taking Saar's hand, he strode off. Eric looked helplessly at Rose. She looked scared. Taking a deep breath, he tried to sound as confident as possible.

"Okay, let's go home." Putting his arm around his sister's shoulder, he followed Weet and Saar down the hill.

The slope was steeper than those they had gone down before, and before long it was cut by narrow, dry ravines. But the going was still easy. The main difficulty lay in avoiding the animals that were intent on going their own way, with no regard for the intentions of the travellers. The small ones were no problem, but when a herd of hadrosaurs appeared, the group had to get out of their way in a hurry.

The extraordinary thing to Eric was the way in which animals that would normally have been mortal enemies now ran side-by-side. The travellers were startled when a party of six velociraptors burst from some bushes to their right and headed straight for them. Instinctively, Eric grabbed Rose and huddled down. Weet turned and began whistling. But the velociraptors ignored both the children and Weet. With hardly a break in its stride, the lead creature leapt over the crouching children, and the others passed close on either side. Farther on, across a large clearing, they saw a huge tyrannosaur fleeing amongst a herd of parasaurolophus. There was no danger of being eaten, but the group had to watch out for being trampled.

They had been travelling for about an hour through the chaos when they came to a narrow gully. It was running west to east and they were on the northern side of it, so it would at least protect them from some of the force of the stampede. Eric was wondering how long this was all going to go on and thinking that a rest would be nice, when Rose interrupted him.

"Look!" she said in an awed whisper, pointing up and to the south.

Eric's heart fell. There were two suns in the sky.

CHAPTER 9

the big bang

"Oh no!" His exclamation stopped the others. Together they stood gazing up at the bizarre sky. As if they too were struck by the sight, the fleeing animals had also stopped and stood in various positions with necks craned and heads tilted, watching.

One sun was where it should be, gently lowering towards the western horizon. The other was larger and far to the south. It was a deep, angry red, and the air around it appeared to be shimmering. Eric thought he could see a black dot at its centre, but the brightness hurt his eyes. He lifted his arm to shield them, but the fireball was too large. The red colour was turning to white and the whole southern sky was becoming unbearably bright.

"This is it," he said helplessly. "This is the big one." Time seemed to stop, but Eric's mind was racing. All his research on the impact seemed to crowd into his brain. The rock was 10 kilometres across and would take about three minutes to travel through the atmosphere before it exploded in the ocean with a force of 75 million megatons, punching a hole 200 kilometres across into the Earth's mantle. In the next weeks, months or years, 75 per cent of all species on the planet would die. What chance did they have?

In eerie silence, the meteor ripped its way through the atmosphere. It appeared to be moving very slowly, yet Eric knew it was travelling at tens of kilometres a second. Everything in the world was frozen by the vision of doom. They were unable to tear their eyes away from the incredibly beautiful sight. Eventually, the fireball slipped over the horizon. The spell broke. Eric noisily let out the breath he had been holding.

"This is it!" he shouted, his voice sounding jarringly loud after the silence. "Into the ravine—quick!"

Grabbing Rose by the arm, he hustled her towards the edge. Weet and Saar were beside him. The southern horizon was a flickering orange. It looked as if the world was on fire.

"Hurry!" he yelled. A low grumbling roar reached the children. It sounded as if it were coming up at them through the ground. Grabbing Rose, Eric thrust her over the lip of the ravine. She tumbled down the side in a cloud of dust. Out of the corner of his eye he saw Weet, Saar and Sinor jump down too. He saw Sally hesitating beside him. With no ceremony, he pushed his pet over the edge and followed her. They tumbled down the slope into an untidy heap. The roaring was getting louder. Gradually, they untangled their limbs. The sound was almost unbearable now, and no-one seemed capable of movement. Rose was crouched down, holding her ears and sobbing. Weet and Saar were hugging each other. Sally was desperately trying to hide in the dirt at the bottom of the gully. Eric sank down and embraced his sister. Would the noise never end?

Suddenly, a blinding flash washed all colour out of the world. But still the noise kept growing. After what seemed an eternity, the noise changed from a dull roar to a harsh, sharp explosion. It was louder than anything Eric had ever imagined. He had heard Weet whistle and knew that sound could hurt, but not this way. His entire body was a mass of pain and his head felt as if it were going to explode. Rose groaned incessantly beside him. Then the sound eased, and an eerie partial silence fell over everything. Eric knew it was just a lull before the blast wave hit. How long did they have, seconds, minutes? He had no idea. Should they move and try to find a safer place? Was there such a thing as a safer place at the end of the world?

Eric remembered a TV show he had seen about a huge meteor hitting New York. He recalled the computer-generated animation of the mushrooming fireball over the eastern USA. The commentator's voice explained that four minutes after impact, skyscraper-sized blocks which had been hurled into space would come raining down on Chicago. Five minutes after that, the same thing would happen to Los Angeles. Eric guessed that southern Alberta was at least as far from the Yucatan Peninsula in Mexico as Los Angeles was from New York. That should at least give them a few minutes to find a better hiding place.

"Come on," he urged, "we have to find somewhere better to hide before the blast wave hits."

Hustling his dazed and unprotesting friends and carrying a shocked Sally, Eric led the way down the ravine. At first the going was difficult and cramped, but soon the ravine deepened and widened and they made better time. Looking at his watch, Eric noticed that five minutes had passed. There was no sign of a good refuge. The ravine walls were smooth red earth and sand which, he felt sure, would collapse in the giant earthquake that was headed their way. The bottom of the ravine was solid rock, and Eric hoped that there would be a hole or cave somewhere in that. The sky above was red and angry, and the air was beginning to feel distinctly warmer. The noise was still there and coming in waves, which varied from a dull background roar to almost unbearably loud thunder. How long did they have?

"Come on," Eric urged them.

"Why? What's the point?" A dispirited Rose sat down on an outcropping of rock.

"We've got to try," said Eric desperately.

"There's no point," his sister continued, "and I'm scared." She looked up at Eric with tears in her eyes and a pleading look on her face. "Let's just wait here. Please."

He didn't know what to say. Rose looked so small and fearful sitting there that he didn't think he had the heart to force her to keep going. And maybe she was right. What was the point of continuing? Eric looked around for his friends. Sinor was pacing back and forth like some nervous bird, Sally lay shivering in Eric's arms. Weet looked dazed. Only Saar appeared okay. Putting an arm around Rose's shoulder, she spoke the first words the children had ever heard her say.

"Weet," she said hesitantly, looking at her partner, "home. I . . . " she tailed off, looking over at Eric and back to Weet. Her words changed to a string of whistles. Weet gazed intently at her for a moment, then turned to Eric. "Saar carry eggs," he said. "We find safe p'ace."

Eric was shocked. Saar had brought eggs over the mountains to the new world. But what sort of world would those young inherit, even if they did survive the next few hours?

"Okay," said Rose, suddenly standing up and assuming her business-like tone. "Come on, Eric, don't just stand around, we have to find a safe place. Let's go."

Rose put her arm around Saar's waist and encouraged Weet to move on. The roaring in the sky swelled again, reminding Eric how little time they had. He glanced at his watch—eight minutes. They had better hurry.

The ravine was still narrow, but was deepening rapidly, and now cut into the solid rock. This encouraged him; they would at least have some protection.

After 12 minutes, Eric was beginning to doubt his hurried calculations. Perhaps his memory was at fault, or maybe the distance was greater than he thought, or else the explosion had not been the impact but a blast in the air. How fast did sound travel?

The course of the ravine was more irregular now, and Eric searched the walls for a cave or an overhang. A loud explosion sounded over the background roar. Eric looked up. The sky was streaked with fire. The fragments thrown into space by the impact were coming back to earth. There were a lot of them, and they were landing with increasing frequency. The explosions were close together, and the ground was shaking.

"Hurry!" Eric yelled, though he doubted if the others could hear him. They were running now and had pulled ahead of him. Eric began running just as they disappeared around a sharp corner in the gully. Tearing around the corner, Eric crashed into Weet's back, dropping Sally to the ground. Staggering to a stop, he looked to see what was holding them up. It was not a sight he wanted to see just then. Standing about 10 metres in front of them was a Tyrannosaurus rex. It was almost too large for the ravine, and stood facing the travellers indecisively. Its head was raised above the lip of the ravine, and it was moving it from side to side. Eric groaned. Worse yet, he could see, behind the monster, a dark patch in the rock wall that he felt sure must be at least a deep overhang. That was their sanctuary, and they couldn't reach it.

"Let us pass," Eric yelled in frustration. "It's all over for you. Don't you understand?"

The tyrannosaurus ignored his pleas. Eric felt a sting on the back of his neck, then another on his hand. He smelled burning and looked down to see a thin tendril of smoke rising from his T-shirt. Sheltering his eyes, he could see that the sky was alive with shooting stars. Millions of them flashed across the heavens, forming a backdrop of fire to the larger streaks of flame left by the meteors. It was like the air itself was burning. Eric could feel the heat on his face. It felt as if he were under a huge gas broiler. A sharp, stinging pain made him wince and brush at his cheek. It was raining dust— hot dust. The particles which had not been thrown high enough to escape the atmosphere and fall back to burn up as shooting stars were falling to earth. Most were very small fragments, but larger rocks occasionally hissed past and bounced at their feet. None of the bigger pieces had hit the travellers yet, but some had made contact with the larger target of the tyrannosaurus. The confused creature was becoming enraged as it was stung by needles of superheated rock. Throwing its head from side to side, it crashed into the wall of the ravine, bringing down a torrent of small stones. Eric saw a chance, their only one.

"Come on!" he screamed, grabbing Sally by her hair and pushing past his friends. Trying not to think of what one of those huge three-toed feet might do if it swung back in his direction, Eric ran as fast as he could. Fortunately, the tyrannosaur was too preoccupied with its own problems to bother with the group, and its bulk even served to protect them from the hot rocks as they scurried past.

Focusing on the black hole in the valley wall, Eric struggled on, driving a panicked Sally in front of him, and pushed his poor pet into the cave. Sinor was next, closely followed by Rose, Weet and Saar. Eric scrambled in last. The smell of burning was strong, and they spent a few moments extinguishing smouldering patches on clothes, backpacks and Sally's hair. At last, the fires were out, and Eric could take stock of their situation. It was not good. Outside the sky still rained fire, heavier now, and the T. rex continued its wild crashings. The cave was not deep, but it was enough for them all to huddle beneath a ledge of solid rock, which gave at least a sense of safety. They could still hear the crashes of meteorites and see the smaller ones bouncing and rolling down the ravine's walls and floor. It was becoming almost unbearably hot.

Rose was the first one to notice the smoke.

"Something's still on fire," she said.

The group checked their clothes and backpacks. There was nothing smouldering, yet the smell was getting stronger. Dark smoke was beginning to drift over the lip of the ravine in front of them. In addition to the crashes, the grumbling of the earth beneath them, and the tyrannosaur's terrorized cries, there was another sound, a loud crackling noise.

"What's that?" asked Rose.

"Trouble," replied Eric, looking at the drifting smoke.

"We're being bombarded by meteorites and you've just realized we're in trouble," Rose sounded scornful.

"Worse than that," said Eric slowly. "We're sheltered from the meteorites, but that noise is a fire. A big one. It must have been started by the hot dust."

Rose sat silently, digesting this information.

"But won't it just burn over the top of us?" she asked at last.

"Yes," replied Eric, "but it'll get very hot and the fire will use up all our oxygen. We'll suffocate."

"Let's run away from it." Rose was moving towards the opening. Eric put his hand on her arm.

"No," he said, "it would be no use. I think the whole world is catching fire."

Rose looked at her brother fearfully and slumped back down. Sweat was dripping from her face, and Sally was panting loudly. No one said a word as they sat listening to the noises from outside and waited for whatever new terror was in store.

CHAPTER 10

the blast wave

The heat was becoming unbearable. It was like slowly baking in an oven.

"This is what a Thanksgiving turkey must feel like," Eric thought bizarrely. Stinging sweat was running into his eyes. When he peered out from beneath the overhang, he could see thick smoke billowing along the lip of the ravine. Farther off, fire darted high in the air where large trees were bursting into flame. The heat was making it difficult to breathe. The air was thin and unsatisfying. The deeper Eric breathed, the more air he needed. The others were having the same difficulty. Sally was lying at his feet, panting shallowly. The crackling was louder now and pieces of black, burned vegetation were drifting into the ravine. The T. rex was roaring loudly, trapped in the narrowing gully; it was too large to continue, too big to turn around, and too stupid to reverse. Eric hugged his sister and hoped for the best.

The best, of course, would have been to suddenly

find themselves in the burger bar in Whistler Village. That didn't happen, but something else did. With virtually no warning, a hurricane burst over the ravine. Flaming trees broke and crashed to the ground, animals were swept helplessly off their feet, even rocks were lifted and carried through the air. The tyrannosaur screamed. Eric caught a glimpse of a world gone mad as he saw things which should have been anchored securely to the earth flying through the red sky. Then everything went black, as something huge blocked the entrance to their small cave.

No one said anything as they sat huddled in the stuffy heat and darkness. They could still hear muffled crashes and groans as the wind whipped over them. At last it stopped and, apart from the now-familiar rumbling on the earth beneath, relative peace returned.

"Are we alive?" Rose was the first to tentatively break their silence.

"I think so," Eric replied. "That must have been the blast wave. We wouldn't have lasted long if we hadn't found this cave."

"Great," said Rose, "but how are we ever going to get out of it?"

It was a good question. Gingerly, Eric leaned forward to where he knew the mouth of the cave should be. He felt a wall of something which felt dry, nobbly and warm. It dawned on him what it was.

"The tyrannosaur," he said. "It must have fallen when the blast hit."

"Is it dead?" Rose asked nervously.

"I think so," Eric replied. He gave the rough skin a hard poke. Nothing happened.

"How are we going to move it?" Another good question from Rose.

"It move," said Weet. He was sitting at the far end of the cave from Eric. His back was against the wall and his feet were pushing against the back of the T. rex. A thin shaft of dull light broke into the darkness from a narrow gap between the dead beast and the cave roof.

"Maybe we can pry a hole and crawl out," Eric said, scrambling over to Weet. Together they placed their feet on the T. rex and pushed as hard as they could. The body moved and the gap grew larger, exposing a dirty, swirling mass of grey. The sky was still streaked with red fire, but the worst of the storm appeared to have passed. A blast of hot, dry air swept into the hole.

Saar joined Weet and Eric, and the hole grew. But whenever they stopped pushing, it closed again.

"Okay," said Weet, "we push, Rose go out."

"I'm not going out there on my own," Rose protested. "There's wind and fire and the T. rex."

"It's okay," Eric said as calmly as he could

manage. "I don't think the T. rex is a problem. The wind has stopped and I couldn't see any smoke or flames when I looked out. Maybe the blast wave blew the fire out. Someone has to go out and see what's happening, and you're the smallest. Come straight back in again if it looks too dangerous."

"Well," Rose sounded uncertain, "will you keep the hole open while I'm outside?"

"Of course we will. Just run out and collect the thickest branches you can carry to prop the hole open. There should be lots lying around after the blast. It'll be fine and soon we'll all be out in the open again."

"All right." Rose still didn't sound totally convinced.

Eric, Weet and Saar pushed again and the hole opened. It was just wide enough for Rose to scramble through. As she wormed her way out, her voice gave a running commentary on the scene.

"Wow, it's a mess out here. There's broken trees everywhere. A lot of them are burned though. It's still windy, but not as bad, and the fire seems to be out. I can't see any animals."

At length she was out and standing on the curve of the T. rex's body.

"Keep the hole open," she warned as she stepped to the side. Eric could still hear her voice.

"The T. rex is dead all right. I'm going to climb

down by the head and. . . AAAHHH!"

"Rose!" Eric screamed and pushed his feet as hard as he could. "What happened? Are you okay?"

For a moment there was no reply, then Rose's voice reached them from farther away: "Yuck, it's horrible. Ugghh."

Barking, Sally scrambled up the T. rex's back and disappeared out the hole to help Rose.

"What is it?" Eric shouted.

"I'm covered in slime. It's gross. I slipped and fell into the T. rex's mouth. Its tongue was all slimy."

Eric breathed a sigh of relief. "Just as well it's dead," he replied as cheerfully as he could.

"It's all right for you," Rose's voice came back angrily. "This is disgust— "

She never finished her sentence. With a deafening roar, the ground bucked sharply and threw Eric against the roof of the cave.

"Rose!" he shouted hopelessly as the body of the T. rex rolled back to plunge them all into deep darkness.

For what seemed like an age, Eric, Weet, Saar and Sinor were thrown painfully around the inside of the cave. It was as if they were trapped inside a dice cup that someone was shaking vigorously. The earth was roaring and crashing as if it were being torn apart. Eric was being beaten black and blue, and he could feel sharper pieces of rock cutting him all over. He tried to curl up into a ball, but the movement of the earth was so violent that he was even beginning to lose track of which way was up. At last he fell, or was thrown upward, and his head made painful contact with a projecting piece of rock. The world inside Eric's head went as dark as the one outside.

CHAPTER 11

eric alone

When Eric came to, the first thing he noticed was the sensation of damp leaves being pressed against his sore head. Opening his eyes, he gazed into Saar's impassive face. It was dirty and covered in scratches and cuts, some still trickling blood. She was cradling his head and pressing a bunch of leaves against an outsized goose egg on his temple. Eric smiled and she nodded. Behind her, he could see Weet watching. He had a large cut on his forehead, and there was blood caked all down the side of his head. From the aches and sharp pains all over his body, Eric doubted if he was in any better shape than his friends.

"Is Rose all right?" Eric asked, remembering the earthquake.

Saar glanced at Weet, but he said nothing. His expression told Eric that all was not well with his sister. Ignoring the pain in his head, he pushed himself into a sitting position. Sinor came into view, looking extremely bedraggled. The group was out of the cave in the middle of the ravine. Most of the ground around was covered with burned, broken branches and rocks. Here and there, the trunks of large blackened trees hung over the lip of the ravine. Tendrils of smoke rose from many of them. The peaceful blue sky of a short while ago was a swirling, angry mass of grey. At the edge of Eric's vision, the grey changed to deep orange, as if somewhere huge fires were casting their glow on the undersides of the clouds. The air was thick with dust and floating flecks of charcoal.

Gingerly turning his head, Eric looked up the ravine. About 50 metres away lay the crumpled body of the T. rex. It lay against the wall, its head bent back at an unnatural angle. On the opposite side was the dark opening of the cave which had saved their lives. Farther up the ravine, one wall had completely collapsed, filling the depression with earth and rock. Nearby, the wall was split open in a jagged crack where the earth had been unable to withstand the forces of the earthquake. It was as dark as if it were twilight, yet he doubted if it could be much past late afternoon. There was no sign of either Rose or Sally.

"Rose!" Eric shouted, struggling to stand. "Where are you? Sally! Here girl."

There was no response. Everything was quiet

and still except for the whispering of the wind above them.

"Where is she?" Eric asked desperately, turning back to Weet. His friend simply shook his head.

"She must be somewhere. Maybe she's hurt."

Eric scrambled away from Saar and crawled awkwardly up the side of the ravine. He ignored the pain in his head and the cuts and bruises which covered his body. Rose was missing. What had happened to her? Was she injured? Did she need help?

The scene that met him at the top of the slope took his breath away. He could see utter devastation in every direction. Hardly a tree still stood. Most lay flat on the ground, their trunks all pointing to the north, away from where the blast wave had come. Those that still stood were blackened, branchless spears, pointing like accusing fingers at the sky. Apart from the debris, dropped when the wind had died, the ground was bare, stripped of all vegetation by the searing heat of the fire and the blast wave. Everything was charred black. Here and there, large lumps indicated the bodies of big animals caught by the fire or the hurricane. On the slope above, a rough new escarpment had been thrown up by the earthquake to almost three times Eric's height. Below him, large bush fires still burned amongst

the lusher vegetation of the plain. There was no sign of the distant silver of the inland sea. Neither was there a sign anywhere that anything other than Eric, Weet, Saar and Sinor had survived the disaster. Rose and Sally had vanished completely.

Eric, joined by Weet and Saar, searched with increasing hopelessness among the fallen trees and rocks. They found not the slightest indication that Rose or Sally had ever been there. At last, the exhausted and shocked trio admitted defeat. Rose and Sally had vanished. Sitting in a bleak huddle, they shared some fruit from Weet's backpack.

"They must have time-travelled," Eric speculated as he bit listlessly into a nan. "Otherwise we would have found something. Wouldn't we?" Eric was thinking out loud to reassure himself. "The earthquake couldn't have made them disappear completely. There were no large holes or big landslides nearby. If they'd been hit by a rock or something, we would have found them."

Eric glanced at Weet, who nodded tiredly. "They go home," he said.

Eric shivered at the thought. What if Rose and Sally had time-jumped and gone home? Why hadn't he? And how was Rose going to explain his absence? Eric's mind was reeling. Why had he been left behind? Was he stuck here forever, doomed to share whatever fate awaited Weet and Saar in this frightening post-impact world? Another thought crossed his mind. What if the skiing accident had been worse than he supposed? What if the blow on the head had killed him? Then he wouldn't be able to go back. Eric felt tears running through the grime on his cheeks. He felt so terribly lonely. Rose could be a pain in the neck, but if he was never going to see her again, he would miss her awfully. Eric clasped his arms around his raised knees and sank his head onto them. Sobs wracked his body. Vaguely, he felt an arm encircling his shoulders and a body pressing comfortingly against his.

Eventually, Eric's sobs subsided. Looking up and wiping his eyes, he saw Saar sitting beside him, looking into his eyes. He smiled weakly. Saar nodded comfortingly. A noise made Eric glance away to where he saw Weet building a fire. It was an easy task. There was broken wood littering the ground and some of the larger tree trunks were still smouldering. Weet was crouched down blowing on some glowing embers. As Eric watched, orange flames danced up brightly and soon a roaring fire was going. Weet dragged up some logs to sit on and the three ate some more fruit and gazed into the flames. It was Weet who broke the silence.

"Rose, Sa"y, go home?" he asked hesitantly.

"Yes," Eric nodded, "I suppose so. That is the only explanation that makes any sense. If there is any sense at all to time travel."

"Why not you?" Weet cocked his head inquiringly to one side.

"I have no idea," replied Eric. "Maybe because we were separated when it happened, or maybe I'm not meant to go back yet." Eric shrugged.

"Maybe fami'y here now. Share home. We find tree ring," said Weet, repeating his earlier offer and blinking his large eyes with the effort of putting so many sentences together.

"Yeah," Eric replied. "If we can find a tree ring standing." He smiled at Weet. His friend's offer to make a home for him here brought him close to tears again. He knew that Weet, and now Saar, would do anything they could for him. He hadn't lost a friend when Weet met Saar, he had gained one. But how would they survive? What would they eat? Where would they sleep? At the thought of sleep, Eric felt incredibly tired. He felt drained, both physically and emotionally. He supposed it was the shock of what had happened.

Looking at his watch, Eric saw that it was still only afternoon, yet it was dark enough to be late evening. All he wanted to do was sleep. After that, he could consider what to do and how to deal with the new situation. Eric slid down and got himself as comfortable as possible against the log.

"Sleep," he said, looking at Weet and Saar. Both

nodded. Weet rose and came over to Eric. He lay down against his left side. Saar lay against his right. Eric felt protected.

"Thank you," he said quietly.

The three lay in silence for a long time, each alone with his or her thoughts.

Weet gazed into the heart of the fire. The glowing embers seemed almost liquid as they wavered and danced before his eyes. He was still stunned by the events of the day. He felt ecstatic that Saar was all right, and yet that emotion made him feel guilty, because his friend Eric had lost Rose. But then Eric might still go back and be reunited with his sister in a world where everything was as it should be. Weet's world would never be the same again.

Weet had come home only to have that home cruelly snatched from him. He glanced across Eric's sleeping body at Saar. What had happened to her home? Had Soron moved the outcasts up onto the escarpment in time? Had they been high enough to escape the waves Eric had predicted would devastate the coast?

Weet was sure those were the questions that were filling Saar's mind right now. He reached over and touched her shoulder reassuringly. At least they had each other. Whatever faced them, they would manage somehow. Regardless of how little Eric and Rose had known of his world, they had never given up. They had faced every new situation bravely, had always found an answer and managed to keep going. That's what he would do, and he would encourage Saar to do the same.

Saar looked over at him. As if she had been reading his thoughts, she whistled that she would always stay with him. If a new world was to be built out of the ruins of the old, they would do it together.

Eric was fast asleep, and Weet felt an irresistible heaviness creep over his tired and sore body. Nestling into a comfortable position, he drifted off into a sleep troubled by nightmares of fire and destruction.

"What on earth possessed the boy to bring a dog onto the ski slopes?"

The familiar voice came to Rose through a veil of pain and confusion. She tried to open her eyes.

"I think Rose is waking up."

With great effort, Rose hauled her eyelids up. Her mother's face hung suspended a metre in front of her.

"How are you feeling? Are you all right? I was

so worried," the face said.

"I think so," Rose managed. "What happened?"

"You and your brother had an argument with a tree, and the tree won," her father said. "We were just coming over to get you for an early lunch, when we saw all three of you pile into this tree. What were you doing bringing Sally onto the slopes anyway?"

"It was Eric," Rose immediately felt defensive. She was saved from further explanation by the intervention of a man in an orange ski suit with the words Ski Patrol across his chest.

"What's your name?" he asked.

"Rose," replied Rose.

"How do you feel?" the man continued.

"I have a headache."

"No dizziness or blurred sight?"

"No," Rose answered.

"What do you remember?" This was becoming like a test.

"Everything," said Rose. And that was true, but she only told the orange man about the ski slope and the accident. Rose knew that if she mentioned even one dinosaur she would end up in hospital fast.

"I think she's fine," the man told Rose's parents. "There is no sign of concussion. Keep an eye on her. If she shows any signs of being overly sleepy, or if she's confused in any way, take her to a doctor, but I don't see anything to be concerned about at the moment."

Confused? That was a joke. How could Rose not be confused? She had just travelled in time and almost been killed by a giant meteorite. Sadly, she wondered what had happened to Weet and Saar. At least, she remembered everything this time, and she could discuss it with Eric as soon as they got the chance. He could be a pain sometimes with all the facts he kept spouting about his beloved dinosaurs, but Rose had to admit that he knew some useful stuff. Where was Eric anyway?

Rose sat up. Sally was sitting close by, looking very sorry for herself and wearing a leash which was held firmly in her father's hand. Rose's mother was kneeling beside her, but she was looking over to where the ski patrol man was crouched over Eric's still form.

"Eric!" she shouted.

"It's okay," said her mother, hurriedly turning back. "He just hasn't woken up yet. He must have hit his head pretty hard." She was trying to sound comforting, but Rose could hear the worry in her voice. The ski patrol man sat back and turned to the family.

"He's still out. As far as I can tell, he only has this bump on his head, but he hit hard and he might not wake up for a little while yet. His breathing and pulse are fine. My guess is that he'll wake up with a really sore head in a couple of hours. Meantime, I'll call for a stretcher and we can take him into the first aid hut. He'll be more comfortable there.

"Don't worry," he added, seeing Rose's mother's look. "He's going to be fine."

CHAPTER 12

home again

The night on the blackened hillside was the worst Eric could remember. He lost count of the number of times he woke up. Apart from the discomfort of sleeping on the ground, there had been aftershocks. Eric didn't know how many, but three had been strong enough to shake him awake. They were accompanied by loud noises from deep within the earth but, even when there was no movement, low grumbling noises came from below, as the planet protested the indignity done to it. Several thunderstorms also passed close by, and although there was no rain, the sound and the brilliant flashes of lightning from the boiling clouds above were enough to wake the three.

Once, Eric woke from a fearful nightmare, in which he had been trapped within an ever-narrowing ring of fire. A break in the clouds above showed a sky alive with the streaks of meteors burning up as they entered the atmosphere. Closer to the horizon, the rolling clouds were lit from inside by lightning flashes and from below by the red glow of some distant fire. It had taken Eric a long time to fall asleep again. He watched the celestial display, worrying about what the future held and wondering where Rose and Sally were.

This trip, he had almost got used to being 65 million years back in time. But it was only now that he realized how much his comfort depended on having Rose and Sally with him. Together they went through adventures and handled all the crises that this strange world could throw at them. Now that Eric was the only human here, he felt adrift and very lonely. If he was going to be trapped here, he would make the best of it, although he didn't relish the thought of trying to survive for long in this bleak place.

He also worried about Weet and Saar. He had known that they might be faced with the destruction of their world, but now that he could actually experience what that meant, it was much harder to deal with. Eric at least had a hope of returning to his future; Weet and Saar were stuck here. Unless Eric found the tunnel, in which case they could follow him through. But what would that mean? If Eric suddenly appeared in the badlands of southern Alberta with three very much alive dinosaurs, what would happen? And how would he explain how they had got there?

What if the tunnel remained open? Scientists would be able to go back in time, but so would journalists, tourists and soldiers. Eric had a vision of the army shooting up hopelessly at Godzilla. It was too much. His tired mind couldn't wrap itself around the problem. Eventually, he dozed off.

He awoke feeling barely refreshed. His body ached, and all the cuts and bruises he had sustained the day before hurt sharply. Weet and Saar were already up and busying themselves around the fire. Thick grey cloud covered the sky and created a sort of twilight. Eric assumed that a slightly brighter patch low to the east marked the position of the sun. It was cold, and a light rain was falling. Eric shivered and stretched his stiff limbs.

"Good morning," he said as cheerfully as he could.

"Good morning," Weet replied. Saar nodded. Together they finished what fruit remained in their backpacks. It wasn't much, but Eric suspected it might be the last decent meal they would have for some time. They ate in silence. When they had finished, Weet pointed downhill and said, "We go?"

"Yes," Eric replied. He could see no alternative to continuing with their original plan and seeing what the future brought. If Weet's estimate had been right, they should be close to the site of his family's tree circle, or what was left of it. From there it would be less than a day to the coast and the tunnel mouth which was Eric's hope for a way home.

Before they set off, Saar used her leaves on the cuts and bruises they had sustained the day before. Every square inch of Eric seemed to hurt, but, after Saar's attentions, he felt a lot better.

Travel through the nightmare landscape was unpleasant. The charred trunks of trees still smouldered and had to be avoided. The rain made the black, muddy ground slick, and everyone was soon filthy from falling down. A more disgusting problem was the carcasses of large animals which lay scattered about. Some of them were beginning to smell, and all attracted a variety of predators, large and small. This included swarms of flying insects, which rose in dark clouds when disturbed. Eric knew that some carried diseases, and he tried to avoid them. That was not always possible, and he couldn't suppress a scream when one large, ugly beetle with a grey body and coppery wings collided with his head and became tangled in his hair. Fluttering angrily, it beat Eric's head with its wings until his wildly flailing arms dislodged it.

The insects were food for a collection of flying

creatures. They were small enough to fit easily on Eric's palm, and all were covered with fur, which gave them a bat-like appearance. Their heads were large for their bodies, with a pair of big yellow eyes. They darted about, catching flying insects between toothed jaws. Eric could hear crunching noises whenever one passed close by.

The larger predators ranged from brightly coloured, toothed birds the size of pigeons to an occasional velociraptor. Eric noticed one Albertosaurus, but no tyrannosaurs. He assumed that the larger the animal, the more likely that it would have been killed the day before. Fortunately, there were enough bodies around that the predators didn't seem interested in chasing live prey such as Weet, Saar and Eric, who were careful to give the feasting packs a wide berth. However, in the half-light, it was sometimes difficult to spot a feeding site, and twice they stumbled on small packs of velociraptors busily eating. In both cases, the carnivores merely hissed a warning, but it was a frightening experience. Visibility grew worse as the day went on. The cloud seemed to be thickening and the sky darkening. By mid-afternoon on Eric's watch, he could no longer make out the sun, and the light was very poor. The air was getting noticeably colder despite the fires, which still cast flickering

red shadows on the undersides of the clouds around them. The rain remained light, although occasional heavy squalls passed over and thunder rolled around the horizon. The squalls were unpleasant, but at least the water washed off some of the dirt.

As they travelled, they came across occasional clumps of bushes which had escaped the chaos of the day before, and from these they picked some fruit to keep them going. Weet took time to inspect anything which could be the remains of a tree ring, hoping for some news of his family, but he had no luck. In one shattered ring, they found two adults and six hatchlings, but they were so shocked that they fled at Weet's approach and didn't respond to his whistled entreaties to return.

At last the bedraggled group reached a river, which Eric hoped was the one he, Rose and Sally had arrived beside during their first visit. It was nothing like the shining, clear water he remembered. It had been reduced to a sluggish brown trickle which wound its torturous way through the snarled mass of charred trees and rocks which almost filled its bed. Nevertheless, it was enough to provide water in which they could wash. This made them feel better, although they were still soaked through and shivering.

"Let's build a fire and warm up," Eric suggested.

Weet hesitated. Eric suspected he would rather continue his search for home, but Saar resolved the dilemma by beginning to collect what dry wood she could and piling it in an area partly sheltered by the remains of a tree ring. Several large trees had been blown over into a jumbled mass. One tree had fallen in a different direction before the previous day's events and had caught the rest. It prevented the other trees from falling all the way to the ground. This created a space beneath the blackened trunks high enough for Weet to stand up in. There were no leaves left, so the branches did not stop the rain completely, but it was better than being in the open, and the ground underneath was less muddy.

There was a lot of wood around, but finding dry twigs was a problem. At last, they built up a respectable fire, and they huddled around it, clothes steaming. It felt good. In the search for fuel, Eric had come across a bush of apps that had escaped the fires. He had picked all the surviving fruit off it, and now they feasted around the blaze.

The food and warmth made them all feel better. Eric began to discuss their position.

"I think," he said, "it might be a good idea to establish a base. We don't know where we are, and there's no use in just wandering around pointlessly like we've been doing all morning. Let's make

‌ ‌

somewhere secure, and then we can search the land from there. At least that way we will always have somewhere warm and dry to return to."

Weet and Saar gazed blankly at their friend. Eric wished Rose was here to understand what he was suggesting.

"Home," Eric tried again, pointing to the fire and the canopy of logs. With a series of gestures, Eric mimed covering the logs to form a roof. Pointing off in different directions he said, "Find family. Bring here." This wasn't a perfect site for a base, but it did have some shelter and a water supply. Weet and Saar looked around and nodded.

"Yes," said Weet, looking from Eric to Saar, "new home."

The rest of the afternoon was spent in making their base more comfortable. There were lots of fallen trees and broken branches, and by placing them carefully between the sloping logs, they managed to create an almost watertight roof. They dragged in some logs for sitting on, and they even managed to create some rough sleeping mats. They were coarse and not very comfortable, but preferable to sleeping on the damp ground. Food was definitely going to be a problem, but for the moment they found enough in sheltered pockets to build up a supply at the back of their new home.

It felt good to be doing something constructive amid so much destruction. Eric was amazed how much better he felt just having such a rough shelter to call home. He knew that predators were going to be a danger as soon as they had finished gorging themselves on the carcasses lying around. Their home would need to be made secure with a wall of trunks and branches in front, but that could wait until tomorrow. For now they had somewhere warm and more-or-less dry to live.

It was evening when they finished, and already so dark that the fire cast flickering shadows on the tree trunks around them. They sat around the fire eating apps, and Eric wondered if the darkness was the beginning of the post-impact winter he had read about. It would be caused by the layer of dust in the atmosphere which had been thrown up by the impact. Some scientists had speculated about a darkness so total that not a single ray of sunlight penetrated for weeks or even months, and that it was this, rather than the impact itself, that had killed most of the dinosaurs. Eric knew that many of the dinosaurs had survived the impact and resultant earthquakes, fires and blast. But, if they were faced with blackness for months, they didn't have a hope. No food would grow, and the weak animals would be susceptible to the diseases Eric had already seen. Those that survived would starve to death. The cold of a world without sunlight would be enough to finish off the dinosaurs, which were not very efficiently warm-blooded. There would also be other unpleasant side-effects, like acid rain and high radiation, when the clouds did eventually clear. Eric shivered and looked at his friends. Weet and Saar were huddled together on a log, and Sinor was sitting looking very sorry for himself at their feet. They were doomed. And so was Eric if he stayed here.

Eric was so wrapped in his misery that he failed to notice their visitors. In fact, it was Sinor who drew their attention to the collection of shadowy figures hovering on the edge of the firelight. Giving a loud whistling chirp, Sinor began pacing and peering into the darkness. It took Eric's eyes a moment to adjust from the brightness of the flames, but there was no mistaking the fact that someone was there. The firelight glinted off almost a dozen pairs of shining yellow eyes.

CHAPTER 13

reunion

Eric, Weet and Saar stared into the darkness. Eric felt terribly vulnerable, exposed in the firelight and not able to see the figures around him. Finally, one of the shadows detached itself and stepped into the light. It was about Weet's height, and Eric would have been hard pressed to tell them apart, except that the stranger had a nasty-looking burned patch on its right shoulder.

The newcomer made whistling sounds, to which Weet responded. After a short conversation, a second figure came forward. This time Weet moved to meet it, and the pair embraced. Turning back to the fire, Weet whistled some words to Saar then, turning to Eric, said one word, "Mother."

Eric's mind raced back to the tree ring and Weet's family from his first visit. He had met Weet's mother then, but he had had trouble telling Weet's mother and father apart. He certainly didn't recognize the figure before him now, but Weet obviously did. Whistling constantly, Weet ushered his mother closer to the fire. Eric and Saar watched as the other figures clustered closer to the warmth.

Eric counted ten newcomers, ranging from hatchlings only a couple of seasons old to full-grown adults. Most were injured in some way, and three had to be supported by their companions, who laid them gently down on the crude sleeping mats. All were covered in dirt and looked around with stunned, vacant expressions. Hesitantly, they shuffled in and arranged themselves around the fire. Eric, Weet and Saar's new home suddenly became very crowded. Saar attended to the most serious injuries. Eric felt helpless until he remembered the food they had collected. The newcomers were mostly sitting now. They accepted his offered apps and nans and began eating listlessly.

All this time, Weet was deep in conversation with his mother and the character with the burned shoulder. When most of the visitors were asleep, either huddled on the sleeping mats or slumped against the logs around the fire, Weet beckoned to Eric and Saar. The three went to the entrance to the shelter and squatted down. Weet had a brief whistling conversation with Saar before turning to Eric.

"Father dead," he said. It sounded strange to

Eric because Weet's voice had no inflection, and his face showed no expression.

"I'm sorry," Eric said.

"They a'ive," Weet swept his arm to indicate the collection of bodies sleeping around the fire. Gradually, with much arm-waving and mime, he told Eric the story.

Two days before, the group had gathered by the sea for the hatching. When the meteorite had struck and the fire had begun falling, they had sought shelter in a deep pool in the river. This, and the protection offered by a high bank, had saved most of them as they huddled in terror. During the earthquake, the bank had collapsed, burying several of them. The rest had to dig them out. These were the three seriously-injured newcomers. When they had eventually emerged from the river bank, the rest of the hatching was gone and fires were raging all around them. Most frighteningly, the sea had vanished entirely, leaving only a flat muddy plain, scattered with the carcasses of stranded marine animals. At this point in the story, Weet pinched his nose and gasped to indicate the stench.

The survivors had spent the next night and day wandering the desolate landscape in shock, avoiding fires and looking for other survivors. They had found none. The fire and the shelter had finally attracted the exhausted group.

Eric glanced around at the pitiful group lying asleep around him. They were all that was left of Weet's people. Perhaps there were isolated individuals living in terror somewhere, like the family they had come across earlier, but Weet's people had become virtually extinct in the blink of an eye. Even if they survived longer, Eric doubted that there were enough survivors to rebuild the species. Most of the newcomers were too old. The eggs Saar carried were a frail hope.

Eric touched his friend comfortingly on the shoulder. Weet, who had been watching Saar, turned and looked at his friend. There was no expression on his face, but Eric somehow knew that Weet realized his people were finished.

"Make new home," Weet said.

Eric nodded. "Yes," he replied. They had to. However hopeless it was, the urge to create hope out of the chaos was irresistible. "We'll make a new home," he continued. "But first we should probably get some sleep."

Weet nodded and went to get some firewood. They built the blaze as high as they dared amidst the crowd of people, and the three friends and Sinor huddled down as comfortably as possible, falling into a troubled sleep.

Unexpectedly, considering what had happened

and the discomfort, Eric slept through the night. He awoke in the bitter cold of what his watch told him must be morning, although there was no sign of the sky lightening. The sound of dripping water had stopped. The rain must be finally over, but it was very cold. Eric was shivering uncontrollably. The fire had almost died down. As he moved his head on his backpack pillow, he remembered his ski suit. Moving quietly so as not to disturb the others, Eric unpacked the suit and put it on. It felt wonderful, although his hands and feet were still painfully cold. Eric tiptoed over the sleeping mass and threw some more wood on the fire. He was rewarded by leaping flames and a welcome wave of warmth. Thinking that he might go and look for some food, he turned to look outside. The sight that met him turned his blood cold. It was a sight familiar to him, but one probably not seen on earth for tens of millions of years. In the flickering light, large, white, soft flakes were drifting down.

"Snow!" Eric was stunned. The flakes were melting on contact with the ground, but there was no mistaking what they meant. In the space of only two days, the climate had changed dramatically. Even a few days of this would mean the end of any creature not fully warm-blooded. Reptiles in Eric's world hibernated to avoid the cold winters, but Eric doubted anything here could adapt quickly enough. How warm-blooded were the dinosaurs? Some of the big ones probably would be finished quickly. Others, like the very active velociraptors, would last longer. How warm-blooded was Weet? He must be warm-blooded to live the life he did, but then Eric remembered how sluggish his friend had been on a couple of slightly chilly mornings.

A frightening thought suddenly came into Eric's mind. He looked around. A few of the figures nearest to the fire were beginning to stir slowly, but the rest were completely immobile. Why, if the cold had woken Eric, had it not woken the others? Eric stumbled back over to where Weet and Saar lay. He took Weet by the shoulders and shook hard.

"Weet! Saar!" he shouted. There was no response. Weet's head lolled awkwardly to one side. Eric panicked. His friend couldn't be dead—not after all they had been through. Grabbing Weet under the arms, Eric dragged him towards the fire. He didn't care if he bumped anyone, but no one complained. Close to the fire, a couple of the newcomers were sitting up, rubbing their arms and legs. Eric pushed between them and laid Weet down as close as he dared to the flames.

Weet felt a sharp pain in his right hand. He knew he had to move it to stop the pain, but it seemed like too much effort. Weet felt as if the earth had sucked him down and was covering him in a thick blanket that wouldn't allow him to move. He opened his eyes.

A glowing log had rolled off the blaze and was lying near his hand. With an immense effort of will, Weet forced himself to move his arm away from the fire. He was beginning to feel better. The side of him that was closest to the fire was feeling warm, and that feeling was starting to move throughout his body. The weight that had seemed to hold him immobile was lifting. He must have been very cold to feel so paralyzed. Weet remembered cold mornings when he had felt that getting up was simply too much effort, but they had been few since he had learned to make fire and had begun wearing tunics of woven creepers. Slowly, Weet moved his left arm to push himself into a sitting position.

Weet had pulled himself upright when he felt a bump on his back. Turning, he saw Eric pulling the still shape of Saar. Slowly, Weet stood to make room, and Eric laid Saar down. One of the strange things about Eric was that the cold didn't appear to affect him. Perhaps his world was colder. Even so, he was wearing the strange second skin in which he had first arrived.

"Thank you," said Weet simply.

"You're welcome," Eric replied, making one of those funny facial movements that Weet found so hard to understand. "Look," he added, pointing away from the fire.

Weet turned his head. It was still dark, but in the flickering light he could see the rain. No, not rain—it was falling much too slowly, and it was falling in large white drops.

"Snow," said Eric.

"Snow," Weet repeated slowly.

This was something new that Eric was familiar with. Did it have something to do with the cold? Weet would have to investigate, but right now he turned his attention to Saar. She was stirring, and her eyes were open. Weet helped her to sit up. Eric moved away and began moving others closer to the heat. Sinor bounded up, not in the least sluggish, and nestled in close to Weet's side. Apparently the cold wasn't bothering him. Weet sighed; there was always something new to discover. Life really was extremely complicated.

CHAPTER 14

T-rex again

Weet and Saar were soon up lending a hand to Eric, who was helping Weet's people get closer to the fire. By the time everyone was taken care of, Eric noticed that there had been a change outside. It had not actually become light, but the darkness was a little less thick. Vague shapes loomed all around, indicating where other fallen trees lay. It was still snowing, but the flakes were slushy now; they would soon turn to rain.

As he sat munching on an app, Eric pondered the situation. The cold added a new complication. He had suspected it would come, but not so quickly. Obviously, it was a serious problem, and something would have to be done. But what?

In the short term, extra fires around their camp would help, and there was plenty of wood lying around. As well, Weet could teach them to weave creepers into tunics, if they could find enough unburned nan plants. But things were only going to get worse. The clouds would get thicker, and it would get colder. The snow was turning to rain this morning, but there would come a day when it didn't. A day when it snowed, and the ground would be cold enough for it to lie. Then they would be immersed in a world of ice that might last for decades.

Eric fingered his ski suit. How he wished he had a dozen of them. The woven tunics would not keep the cold out very well, and there were no large furry animals whose skins could be used for clothes. Any way he looked at it, Eric could not see an answer. Weet and what was left of his world were doomed to a slow extinction. Eric's emotions were very confused. On the one hand, his friends and this strange world he had come to love were finished. On the other, the end of Weet's world allowed the evolution of his own. If the fires and the darkness and cold hadn't come, Eric and Rose would never have been born.

Somewhere beneath his feet, there were small, furry, rodent-like creatures. They were living on the roots of the burned trees and bushes and on the water which trickled down from the melting snow. They were secure and only vaguely aware of the catastrophe being played out above them. In weeks, or months, or years, when the sun had returned, and when the acid rain had washed away, and when new plants were springing up all over, they would emerge into an empty world. There would be no competing dinosaurs to chase them back into their holes, and they would spread out and thrive. Over millions of years, they would evolve into a whole range of weird and wonderful creatures. The weirdest and most wonderful of these would be a small ape which one day would climb down from the trees and begin walking on its back legs. Over more millions of years, that odd ape would learn to tame fire and dogs, to build shelters, to hunt and farm, to talk and write, to build cities and cars and factories. In time, the ape would examine its own past and wonder at the bones of the extraordinary animals which had vanished long before.

Eric sighed. If he succeeded in finding his way home, it would be hard to leave. He would always feel he had deserted his friends, but he had no choice. His world was where Rose and Sally and his parents and his school and his future were and, somehow, he would have to say good-bye to Weet and Saar.

Eric's thoughts were interrupted by the approach of Weet and Saar.

"More fire," Weet said, sweeping his arm to encompass the camp.

"Yes," agreed Eric, "and more food too. There are a lot of mouths to feed now." Weet nodded.

"We 'ook," he said, indicating the survivors around the fire, who had organized themselves into pairs. The injured three were still lying on the sleeping mats, but the rest were obviously ready to go off in search of food and firewood.

"You go home?" The question took Eric by surprise.

"What?" he asked.

"You go home?" Weet repeated. "We find tunne'. You go home Rose and Sa''y."

Eric felt a lump forming in his throat. This is what he had been planning to do, but what had been difficult was the thought that he would be betraying Weet by leaving him. Now, here was Weet suggesting the same thing.

"Yes," said Eric. "I will go home. If I can."

Weet nodded again. "They," he said, indicating the other survivors, "gather food. Saar stay with sick. Weet he'p Eric home."

Eric felt his eyes water. "I could stay and help," he said with difficulty.

"No." Weet stared at Eric. "I home," he said firmly. "I he'p my peop'e." He pulled himself up to his full height, towering over his friend. "I am Weet."

Eric could feel the hot tears running down his cheeks. Stepping forward, he embraced his friend. "Yes, you are," he choked softly.

Weet and Eric were the last pair to leave. The others had set off in different directions, the fittest to go far and search for food sources, the rest to stay close and bring in wood for burning. Saar would stay to keep the fire alight, and to tend to the three injured survivors. Eric hugged Saar before they left.

"Good-bye," said Eric, even though he knew Saar couldn't understand him. "When I first met you, I thought you were going to take my friend away from me. Now I see that I have gained a new friend. I'll always remember you." Saar nodded at Eric. Then the pair stepped out into the rainy darkness.

Eric and Weet, with Sinor dancing at their heels, followed the course of the river down towards the shore of the sea. The going was made difficult by fallen trees, which had to be scrambled over or walked around. Eric could only see about a metre ahead. The darkness was that of a moonless night, except there was no sign of any stars. The far-off glow of some large fires which were still burning cast eerie orange shadows on the undersides of the clouds, but did nothing to relieve the gloom around them. If the clouds kept on thickening, as Eric suspected they would, in a day or two it would be totally black. Then travel across any distance would become virtually impossible. How would Weet and his people collect what sparse food remained?

Mostly, they walked in silence, still stunned by the horrors of the previous two days. Once, when they were resting on a blackened log, Weet's words again brought Eric to the edge of tears.

"Weet home gone," he said abruptly.

"No," Eric insisted instinctively, "you'll manage. There is some food. You'll find more survivors and rebuild your tree rings. And there are Saar's eggs. They will hatch into a new generation."

Eric didn't know whether Weet understood, but his friend just shook his head.

"The end," he said. "Soon Weet, Saar, Sinor," he reached down and patted his pet's head, "just be" —he hesitated and looked hard at Eric—"just be bones."

"No!" Eric cried, but he knew it was true. Had he done Weet a favour by making him aware of the fate that lay in store for all his people? He couldn't think of anything else to say. Reaching out, he rested his hand on his friend's shoulder.

"But Eric," he said, placing his thin three-fingered hand over his companion's, "you go home. Thank you for coming here; te"ing me of your wor'd—and mine. We had. . . " he hesitated, searching for the right word.

"Fun," said Eric helpfully.

"Yes" continued Weet, "we had fun. I 'earn. You 'earn. Whatever next, we not 'ose other now."

"No," agreed Eric, "we won't lose each other now."

The pair sat side by side in silence for a long time before continuing their trek. Eric walked in a kind of daze, his thoughts full of images of his friend and the fate that awaited him. He was jerked out of his depressing reverie by an unseen root which caught his foot and threw him to the ground. The padding on his ski suit protected him from injury, but he let out a cry of surprise. Weet came over and offered him a hand up. That probably saved both their lives. As Eric regained his feet, a large dark shadow rose before them. Eric recognized the shape, and the roar confirmed the presence of the first tyrannosaur they had seen since the impact. It had been lying in their path and, if it had not been disturbed by Eric's cry, the pair would probably have stumbled right into it. Now it rose and towered over them.

"Don't move," Eric whispered unnecessarily. Even Sinor had frozen in place. Eric could hear the T. rex grunting and snuffling over the soft hiss of the rain, which was falling steadily now. The creature was obviously confused, partly by the cold, although its large bulk would have prevented its body from cooling down too quickly, and partly by the darkness and chaos. Eric doubted it could see them, and its sense of smell was probably upset by the rain and the burned smell which was everywhere. As Eric's eyes made out the shape of the beast, he noticed that the tyrannosaur was leaning over to one side, as if favouring its right leg. Looking hard, Eric could discern a darker mark on its thigh. It was injured. That might explain why it wasn't feeding on the carcasses that were lying around.

Eric was busy trying to work out a way in which they could sneak away and go around the T. rex when Sinor became bored. Concluding that there was no danger, he rushed forward to torment the injured animal.

"No," Eric shouted instinctively, "leave it alone."

But Sinor continued, whistling in a high-pitched tone and dancing around the T. rex's feet. Confused, the animal shuffled around on its good leg, craning forward to see what was happening at its feet. The effort was too much. The thick tail swung up and waved wildly in an attempt to regain balance, but the injured leg couldn't hold enough weight.

"It's falling!" Eric screamed as the huge shape loomed over them. Grabbing Weet by the arm, Eric dragged him aside, hoping desperately that there were no more roots in that direction. With an earth-shaking crash, the T. rex hit the ground only centimetres behind Weet. Still struggling away, Eric caught a glimpse of a red eye and a familiar collection of steak knife teeth clacking open and shut behind him. Warm, foul breath washed over him. Then they were clear.

Scrambling over a log, Eric crouched down and looked back. Weet was beside him, and Sinor was prancing triumphantly along the top of the log. The T. rex was breathing heavily and twisting its body in a vain attempt to roll over and get its short front legs beneath it so it could lever itself upright again. It was not having much success. Fearsome killer though it was, Eric felt sorry for it, struggling against forces it could never understand. In a matter of days, it had been reduced from the most fearsome predator the world had ever seen to a helpless, jerking form gasping in the darkness. Eric sighed.

"Sinor," he said quietly, "that wasn't fair." Sinor cocked his head at Eric, but continued his victory dance on the log. "Come on," Eric added, "let's keep going."

CHAPTER 15

the eating ground

About an hour after they had encountered the T. rex, they arrived at what had been the sea. The trickle of the river seeped onto a dark, muddy plain. Eric's bare feet, which had suffered a bit on his recent journeys, squelched into thick black mud. Ankle deep, the mud seemed to be trying to suck him down, and only released him reluctantly, with a loud plop. The pair couldn't see very far and headed out to investigate. They went some distance with no sign of water before an encounter with the slimy body of some stranded sea creature persuaded them to retreat.

Eric led the way along the bank towards where he hoped to find the entrance to the tunnel that had first brought him to Weet's world. They had not used it to return on the first visit, because the mouth had caved in, and because the slippery bank had been unclimbable. That might still be the case, but the landscape had changed, and this was the only hope Eric had of returning to Rose and Sally.

As they progressed, Eric recognized nothing. The darkness and the lack of vegetation made it all look the same. After about half an hour's walking, Eric was convinced that they had passed the entrance to the tunnel. He thought he remembered it only taking them a few minutes to reach the river. He was fairly sure it was the same river, but there was not the slightest sign of any opening in the uniformly black, slimy bank. Retracing their steps back to the river didn't help. It was hopeless. Eric slumped down in the mud. This had been his only hope. Now what was left to do?

"No tunne'?" Weet asked.

Eric shook his head. "No," he replied, "or if there is, it's covered over so well we'll never find it. Even if we did find it, there is no guarantee that the tunnel would be open. The passages between your world and mine aren't simply open all the time. They seem to depend on circumstances."

Eric felt a hand on his shoulder. "You go home soon," Weet said comfortingly. Then Eric felt the hand go tense. A high, sharp cry echoed from the darkness. It was Sinor, and he was in trouble.

Running as fast as the clinging mud would allow, the pair hurried towards the sounds. Eric was the first to see the struggling shape of his friend's pet.

"There he is," he shouted as he headed for Sinor.

The closer he got, the thicker the mud seemed to be and the slower he progressed. It began to feel as if he were running in molasses. But he was almost there. Sinor seemed to be stuck in the mud. He was struggling violently, but not getting anywhere.

Eric had almost reached Sinor, but the mud was over his ankles and he couldn't move easily. He heard Weet whistling behind him, but ignored him. Falling to his knees, Eric reached forward and managed to grab Sinor. The animal was not heavy, but he was trapped up to his body in the mud. Eric pulled, but all that happened was that his own knees sank farther into the mud. Sinor had calmed down when he felt Eric's hands on him, but a straight pull was only going to hurt him. Eric began rocking Sinor back and forth to try and weaken the mud's grip. It worked, but the rocking motion pushed Eric deeper down. Ignoring what was happening to himself, Eric continued working. Sinor kicked his legs to help free them. At last, with a loud sucking sound, he popped free.

Eric held him close to his chest and tried to turn. The mud was above his knees now. Because he had knelt to reach Sinor, his legs were bent backwards and Eric couldn't get enough leverage to push himself free. Twisting around, he saw Weet standing a metre away. The mud was over his feet.

"Eating ground," he explained. The term didn't encourage Eric.

"Can you reach Sinor?" the boy asked.

Very slowly, Weet edged forward. His feet sank deeper.

"Stop!" Eric shouted. "I don't want us all stuck. I'll throw Sinor. You catch him." Eric made throwing motions and Weet halted. Clutching Sinor firmly, Eric twisted back and forth, counting loudly. "One! Two! Three!"

On the count of three, Eric swung around and launched Sinor towards Weet. Sinor whistled in fear and scrabbled at the air with his feet, but Weet caught him cleanly against his chest.

"Good catch," said Eric. He watched as Weet carefully retreated. When he was on firm ground, he placed Sinor down beside him and faced Eric again. Even though he was standing close by, he was only a silhouette of deeper darkness against the background.

"I go," he whistled. Eric watched with a sinking heart as the dark figure retreated. After a few steps, it was swallowed by the blackness. Eric was puzzled. Why was Weet deserting him? Why wasn't he helping him out? All his exertions to throw Sinor had sunk him deeper. The mud was up to his thighs now and felt as if it were holding him in a vice. Slowly, Eric tried to pull one leg up.

The other sank deeper. He reversed the process and the opposite happened. The mud continued to creep up. It felt like a cold blanket wrapped around his legs. But someone was pulling on the blanket, slowly sucking him down.

Eric felt the first shiverings of fear. Everything he had heard about quicksand rushed back into his mind. This was mud, not quicksand, but the effect was the same. Eric felt himself slowly sinking. Images of doomed explorers disappearing forever out of sight flashed before him. What was it you were supposed to do in quicksand? Did lying flat slow the sinking down or speed it up? He couldn't remember. A wave of panic swept over him and he struggled to free his legs. The more he struggled, the deeper he sank. The mud was almost at his waist now.

"Stop!" he shouted at himself in an effort to calm down. Struggling just made you sink faster. With an incredible effort, Eric forced down the waves of panic and made himself breath steadily. He must stop struggling. The feeling of the cold, black mud slowly and inexorably creeping up his body was horrible, but the movement was slower now that he was still. What could he do? Where was Weet?

"Eric!" Very carefully, he turned his upper body. Weet's figure was silhouetted against the gloom. Sinor was at his feet, and he was carrying a long stick. "I pu'' you," he said.

"Okay," Eric replied. He felt relieved that his friend had not deserted him. The panic receded. Gingerly, Weet circled Eric until the boy didn't have to twist his body painfully to face him. Then he edged forward and reached out as far as he could. Eric could just grab the end of the stick. The feel of its solid security linking him to his friend was comforting.

Gradually, Weet began to pull. Eric could feel the strain of his body pulling against the sucking mud. He was moving. His feet and legs were still held firm, but his upper body was inclining towards Weet. The mud was creeping up his chest as he was pulled forward, and his arms ached with the strain. Weet was leaning back, his feet digging into the mud, arms straining with the effort.

Eric's body was now in line with the stick. He was having trouble keeping his face out of the black ooze, but he was feeling upward movement. The mud seemed to be loosening its grip. Eric tried kicking his legs. There was not a lot of movement, but he was getting free. A surge of hope swept through him. Then the stick jerked and went loose. Looking up, Eric saw Weet lying on his back in the mud. His feet had slid from under him, and he had fallen. The mud reasserted its grip on Eric like a giant hand closing around his body. It was holding him tighter than ever and seemed to be pulling him down again.

"Weet," Eric cried, "are you okay?"

Weet scrambled and slithered back to his feet. "Okay," he said, grabbing onto the stick.

It had only taken moments for Weet to regain his feet, but in that time Eric had been sucked further down. The mud was up to his armpits and it seemed to be softer than before, pulling him in faster. Eric tightened his grip on the stick. Weet pulled again, but nothing happened. After a while, Weet gasped and relaxed. Eric had not budged a millimetre. In fact, as soon as the strain was released, Eric sank farther into the slime. Now it was up to his chin. Weet pulled again. Eric could hear his heavy breathing, and he felt as if his arms were about to pop out of their sockets. But still nothing happened. The hand beneath the ground held him fast and was inexorably sucking him in.

Eric tried to shout and got a mouthful of foul-tasting mud. Spitting, he screamed, "Weet! It's no use. Keep back!"

Weet dropped the stick and threw himself flat onto the mud. He could almost reach Eric's outstretched hand.

"It's no use," the boy repeated. "Good-bye, Weet."

"Good-bye, Eric. Thank you."

The cold mud was filling Eric's ears now. He

only had time to gasp a last lung full of air before it filled his mouth, his nose and oozed over his closed eyes. Eric's head was completely buried now, and still the mud was clutching him and pulling him remorselessly down. His lungs hurt as the air in them was used up and they cried out for more. Eric's right hand was still in the open air and the last thing he felt, before the blackness completely overcame his senses, was another hand, a three-fingered hand, grasping his and squeezing it.

CHAPTER 16
the return

Eric was still struggling and fighting the grip of the mud, and the weight was still on his legs. He kicked tentatively. He could move. He had to get rid of the weight. Eric pulled his legs up and kicked as hard as he could. The weight left him. He was free! Thankfully, he gasped in a huge lung full of fresh air.

"Nurse! Nurse!" A familiar voice screamed close to his ear.

A door slammed, and another voice joined in. "He's coming out of it. It's alright. Calm down. You'll be fine. Calm down."

Eric felt hands on him, soothing him, calming him. Gradually, he relaxed.

"Eric!" It was Rose's voice. "Open your eyes."

Eric tried. Slowly his lids slid up. It was bright. Painfully bright after the darkness of the mud. Everything was white instead of black. Was he dead? Was he in heaven? With an immense effort, Eric turned his head. There was an angel, dressed in white and smiling down on him. But where were her wings?

"Where am I?" Eric asked weakly.

"Foothills Hospital," said the smiling angel. "You've been unconscious for a week. Welcome back." She busied herself pulling up the sheets and blankets Eric had kicked off.

"Thank you," said Eric politely. Turning his head the other way, he saw Rose. "Hello, Rose," he added, smiling.

"Hello, Eric," replied his sister. "I'm glad you woke up. Mom and Dad are really worried. They only left to go to the cafeteria for lunch."

"I'll page them in a minute," the nurse interrupted. "How do you feel?"

"Good," Eric replied, turning back. "Have I really been out for a whole week?"

"Yes," came the answer. "After your skiing accident, you refused to wake up. They couldn't find anything wrong with you in Vancouver, so we decided it would be best to medi-vac you back to Calgary, so you could be close to home. You arrived yesterday. Do you have a headache, or any other aches and pains?"

"No," Eric shook his head slowly.

"How about dizziness? Do you feel dizzy?"

"No," Eric replied again. "But I do feel a bit hungry," he added.

The nurse laughed. "Okay. I'll see if I can organize some food for you. I'll send the doctor in to check you over as well. Right now, I'd better tell your parents that you've rejoined us."

"Thank you," said Eric as the nurse headed for the door.

"Rose," he asked urgently as soon as the nurse had left the room. "Do you remember?"

"Yes," said Rose, "I remember this time too."

"What happened to you in the earthquake?"

"I don't know," Rose replied. "One minute I was in the gully covered in T. rex slobber," she shivered at the memory, "then I was back on the ski slope. We were really worried about you. The Ski Patrol took you to the first aid hut and then, when you still wouldn't wake up, they called an ambulance and we all went to the Vancouver General. Mom and Dad were frantic. The doctors spent two whole days doing every test they could think of, but they couldn't find anything wrong. Then they decided it wouldn't hurt to move you, and it would be better for everyone if you were back in Calgary. So you and Mom flew back on a medi-vac. Dad and I had to drive." Rose frowned as if she were jealous of his flight. Then she continued, "So that's what happened here. What happened back in Weet's time? How is he? Did everyone survive the earthquake?"

"Whoa!" Eric held his hand up. "One question at a time." Then he told Rose everything that had happened. When he finished, Rose sat in silence for a minute.

"Being sucked down into quicksand must have been really scary," she said eventually. "What do you think will happen to Weet and Saar?"

"I don't know," said Eric thoughtfully. "Weet is organizing the group. If there is any hope, Weet and Saar will cope."

Eric fell silent. There was no hope. He knew that. Weet, Saar and the others might manage for days, weeks, months, or even years, but their species would die out. He also knew that his part in the story had ended. They would never time-jump again. His life was in this world from now on, and that was fine with him. Eric had grown up a lot in his three visits to Weet's world, perhaps more than he would have wished, but it was over now.

"I don't think we'll go back again," he said gently, not sure of Rose's response. As always, it surprised him.

"Oh, I know that," she said dismissively. "As soon as I woke up on the ski slope, I knew that was the end. Don't you feel that?"

Eric thought for a minute. Yes, he did know that. Each time before, there had been a feeling of unfinished business. Now, the story was complete.

"Yes," he agreed, "I do feel that this time. What I'm not sure about is why we went back at all. I thought all along that it was to tell Weet what was going to happen to his world, but if that was the reason, why didn't we come back as soon as we told him? Why did we have to go through the impact and the earthquake?"

"I think I know," Rose's face took on her very serious look as she concentrated on putting her thoughts into words. "We always thought that we went back to help Weet, to teach him to make fire or tell him about the meteorite, but I don't think that's right. I think we went back so Weet could teach us something."

"What?" Eric stared at his sister. "What do you mean?"

"Well," she continued slowly, "we've both changed. You used to be such a pain about your dinosaurs."

"What do you mean?" Eric interrupted again defensively.

"You always seemed to be telling me stuff, whether I wanted to hear it or not. I liked dinosaurs, but I could never admit it. They were your thing and you were always talking about them, and not giving anyone else a chance. Now that you've met them, you're much easier to talk to. You still know a lot, but you don't ram it down my throat any more."

Eric was silent for a minute. It was true. He had to admit it. Now he wouldn't feel the need to show everyone how much he knew.

"You've changed too," he told Rose. "You don't throw tantrums like you used too. I used to be scared about how you would react to anything I told you, in case it would turn into a fight. Now we can talk about things."

Rose nodded. "I guess that's growing up." The pair grinned at each other. "We can thank Weet for that, wherever, or whenever, he is."

"You're awake!" The children's mother burst into the room, closely followed by their father. "We were so worried. How are you feeling? The nurse said you were fine. Has the doctor been in yet?" She bustled around the bed in concern, stroking Eric's hair and straightening his sheets.

"Not yet," Eric managed to reply to the last question. "I'm fine Mom, really."

"You did give us quite a fright," Eric's Dad stepped forward, smiling. "That trip turned into quite the adventure." Eric laughed. He turned to Rose and winked broadly. "Yes, it did," he said.

Weet slithered backward through the clinging mud and stood up. He could still feel the pressure of Eric's hand in his, but there was no sign of his friend. The eating ground in front of him was as smooth as if nothing had ever disturbed it. He sighed. It was over. He knew with certainty that he would never see either his friends or their dog again. He felt alone, but of course he wasn't; he knew that too. There was Saar and the eggs she carried, and the other survivors who were looking to him for leadership in this difficult new world. He would do the best he could to help them all survive through whatever came next. Eric had taught him many things which would help. The most important was to never give up in the face of whatever the world threw at you.

"Good-bye, Eric," Weet used the strange language of his friends for the last time. Then he straightened, whistled to Sinor, and set off across the mud, back to Saar and the others and life in a forever-changed world.

THE END

AUTHOR'S NOTE

Did the dinosaurs really die out in the unimaginable flash of an intergalactic collision? Probably.

The crater has been found, a 200-kilometre circle of tortured rock buried beneath the Yucatan Peninsula in Mexico. It is called Chicxulub (pronounced shicks-you-loob) and marks where a meteorite or comet fragment 10 kilometres across landed at exactly the right time. The impact dug a hole through the earth's crust and into the mantle and threw up dust, ash, molten rock and rocks. On the surface of the earth, it left a layer of very distinctive clay, only a few centimetres thick but traceable in rocks right around the world. Below this clay layer, there are dinosaurs; above it, there are not.

The clay layer represents the impact that killed the dinosaurs. But how?

Obviously, if you were a T. rex standing where the Yucatan peninsula is now, you would have been vapourized, along with the meteorite and a sizable section of the Earth's crust. But what if you were a hadrosaur placidly grazing on the opposite side of the planet? It might have been the earthquakes, or the continent-wide fires started by the molten rock falling back through the atmosphere, or the giant tidal waves which were probably hundreds of metres high, or the darkness as the ash blanketed the Earth and cut off your sunlight for weeks, months, or years. Or it might have been the acid rain, or the radiation bombarding you through what was left of the ozone layer, or a combination of all of them.

No one knows for sure. And there are problems.

All the dinosaurs died out, along with all the flying reptiles, most of the large marine reptiles, a lot of birds, plants, plankton—in fact, 75 per cent of all life on Earth. So why not the other 25 per cent? Any explanation of why the dinosaurs died out must also explain why sharks, crocodiles, turtles, birds, and a host of other flying, crawling, burrowing and swimming animals and the plants they fed on carried on as if nothing had happened.

Even with the dinosaurs themselves it is not clear. Some studies show that as you look at rocks closer to the clay layer that marks the impact, there are fewer and fewer dinosaurs and not as many different species. Maybe the climate was changing (studies of plants suggest the weather was getting colder as the end approached). This could have been caused by small meteorite impacts like the Fire Nights, but there are other possibilities.

Maybe a new land link between America and Asia was allowing the different species of dinosaurs to mix (like the arrival of the velociraptors in Weet's world) and spread disease or the bugs that carried disease.

There is no simple explanation, and because we can only look at the rocks, we only see a part of the picture. If we could travel back in time like Eric and Rose, the situation would certainly seem as complex as it did to them.

WILSON

ABOUT THE AUTHOR

John Wilson lives on Vancouver Island with his wife and three children. After a career as a geologist in Scotland, Zimbabwe and Alberta, John began writing in 1989. His freelance work and poetry have appeared in many newspapers and magazines, and his children's stories in *Chickadee*. His other books for young people are the novels *Weet*, which begins the adventures of Eric, Rose and Sally, *Weet's Quest* (both available from Napoleon Publishing), *Lost in Spain* (Fitzhenry and Whiteside) and *Across Frozen Seas* (Beach Holme Publishing), a novel about the Franklin Expedition. He is also the author of an adult book on the same topic, *North With Franklin: The Lost Journals of James Fitzjames* (Fitzhenry and Whiteside), and a young adult biography of Norman Bethune, *Norman Bethune: A Life of Passionate Conviction* (XYZ Publishing).